A... My Name is Alice

A Musical Review

Conceived by

Joan Micklin Silver
and Julianne Boyd

SAMUEL FRENCH
FOUNDED 1830

New York Hollywood London Toronto

SAMUELFRENCH.COM

ISBN 978-0-573-68177-6   Printed in U.S.A.   #3647

ACT I:

ALL GIRL BAND
Lyrics by David Zippel; Music by Doug Katsaros Copyright 1983 David Zippel and Doug Katsaros/All rights reserved.

A . . . MY NAME IS ALICE POEMS
By Marta Kauffman & David Crane Copyright 1984 Crane & Kauffman/All rights reserved.

AT MY AGE
Lyrics by June Siegel; Music by Glen Roven. Copyright 1983 Roven & Siegel/All rights reserved.

TRASH
Lyrics by Marta Kauffman & David Crane; Music by Michael Skloff· Copyright 1984 Skloff, Crane & Kauffman/All rights reserved.

FOR WOMEN ONLY POEMS
By Marta Kauffman & David Crane· Copyright 1984 Crane & Kauffman/All rights reserved.

GOOD THING I LEARNED TO DANCE
Lyrics by Mark Saltzman; Music by Stephen Lawrence: Copyright 1983 SJL Music Co./All rights reserved.

WELCOME TO KINDERGARTEN, MRS. JOHNSON
Lyrics by Marta Kauffman & David Crane, Music by Michael Skloff Copyright 1984 Skloff, Crane & Kauffman/All rights reserved

I SURE LIKE THE BOYS
Lyrics by Steve Tesich, Music by Lucy Simon: Copyright 1984 Sigh & Moan/All rights reserved

MS MAE
By Cassandra Medley. Copyright 1984 Cassandra Medley/All rights reserved

GOOD SPORTS
"DETROIT PERSONS"
By Susan Rice
"EDUCATED FEET"
By Carol Hall Copyright 1984 Daniel Music LTD/All rights reserved.

THE PORTRAIT
Lyrics & Music by Amanda McBroom Copyright 1981 McBroom Music Used by permission. All rights reserved

BLUER THAN YOU
Lyrics by Winnie Holzman, Music by David Evans Copyright 1983 Holzman & Evans/All rights reserved.

ACT II·

PRETTY YOUNG MEN
Lyrics by Susan Birkenhead, Music by Lucy Simon Copyright 1984 Calougie Music & Algebra/All rights reserved

DEMIGOD
By Richard LaGravanese Copyright 1984 Richard LaGravenese/All rights reserved.

THE FRENCH SONG
Lyrics & Music by Don Tucker, Monologue by Art Murray· Copyright 1977 Murray & Tucker/All rights reserved

3

TOP OF THE GATE

(The Village Gate)
160 BLEECKER STREET

Rosita Sarnoff, Anne Wilder and Douglas F. Goodman
present

A . . . MY NAME IS ALICE

A New Musical Revue
starring
Roo Brown
Randy Graff
Mary Gordon Murray
Alaina Reed
Charlaine Woodard
with material by

Calvin Alexander	Georgia Bogardus Holof	Anne Meara	James Shorter
Susan Birkenhead	Winnie Holzman	Cassandra Medley	June Siegel
Maggie Bloomfield	Doug Katsaros	David Mettee	Lucy Simon
David Crane	Marta Kauffman	Art Murray	Michael Skloff
David Evans	Richard LaGravenese	Susan Rice	Steve Tesich
Carol Hall	Stephen Lawrence	Glen Roven	Don Tucker
Cheryl Hardwick	Amanda McBroom	Mark Saltzman	David Zippel

set design by	costume design by	lighting design by	sound design by
Ray Recht	Ruth Morley	Ann Wrightson	Tom Gould

orchestrations by	musical director	associate producers
Doug Katsaros	Michael Skloff	Frederick D Offenberg
		Mark Teschner

casting	originally produced by	stage manager
Elissa Myers Casting	The Women's Project	Renee F Lutz
	at the American Place	
	Theatre	

Choreography by

Edward Love

conceived and directed by

Joan Micklin Silver and Julianne Boyd

MUSICAL NUMBERS AND SCENES

ACT I

ALL GIRL BAND 9
Lyrics by David Zippel; music by Doug Karsaros
A ... MY NAME IS ALICE POEMS 11
by Marta Kauffman and David Crane
AT MY AGE 12
Lyrics by June Siegel; music by Glen Roven
TRASH................... 15
Lyrics by Marta Kauffman and David Crane
Music by Michael Skloff
FOR WOMEN ONLY POEMS 18
by Marta Kauffman and David Crane
GOOD THING I LEARNED TO DANCE 19
Lyrics by Mark Saltzman; music by Stephen Lawrence
WELCOME TO KINDERGARTEN, MRS. JOHNSON 21
Lyrics by Marta Kauffman and David Crane
Music by Michael Skloff
I SURE LIKE THE BOYS 24
Lyrics by Steve Tesich; music by Lucy Simon
MS. MAE...... 25
by Cassandra Medley
GOOD SPORTS:
DETROIT PERSONS 28
by Susan Rice
EDUCATED FEET 30
by Carol Hall
THE PORTRAIT 32
Lyrics and music by Amanda McBroom
BLUER THAN YOU .... .34
Lyrics by Winnie Holzman; music by David Evans

ACT II

PRETTY YOUNG MEN 37
Lyrics by Susan Birkenhead; music by Lucy Simon
DEMIGOD 40
by Richard LaGravenese
THE FRENCH MONOLOGUE ... .41
by Art Murray
THE FRENCH SONG 41
Lyrics and music by Don Tucker
PAY THEM NO MIND 42
Lyrics and music by Calvin Alexander and James Shorter

HOT LUNCH 44
by Anne Meara
EMILY THE M.B.A. 47
Lyrics by Mark Saltzman; music by Stephen Lawrence
SISTERS 51
Lyrics by Maggie Bloomfield; music by Cheryl Hardwick
HONEYPOT 52
Lyrics by Mark Saltzman; music by Stephen Lawrence
FRIENDS..56
Lyrics by Georgia Holof; music by David Mettee
ALL GIRL BAND (Reprise) 59
Lyrics by David Zippel; music by Doug Katsaros

A . . . My Name is Alice

The house lights go down and the stage is dark. Lights come up as the FIRST ACTRESS enters c. stage. As the song progresses the dancing becomes spirited, reminiscent of a syncopated marching band.

ALL-GIRL BAND

First Actress.
IT WAS ONE OF THOSE DAYS
WHEN YOUR MIND IS A MAZE.
I WAS TRAPPED IN THE DOUBT OF MY LIFE.
  Second Actress. (*enters from* us.c.)
I WAS DOING A QUIZ
FOUND IN *COSMO* OR *MS.*
WHEN THE MUSIC WENT OUT OF MY LIFE.
  Both.
BUT I'M NOT THE TYPE TO FACE THE BLUES ALONE.
  First Actress.
SO I DUSTED OFF MY FLUTE.
  Second Actress.
AND SLIDE TROMBONE —
  Both.
AND JOINED AN ALL-GIRL BAND.
NOW I JAM FROM THE NIGHT TILL THE MORN.
I JOINED AN ALL-GIRL BAND.
NOW I CAN BLOW MY OWN HORN!
  Third Actress. (*enters c. stage*)
I WAS FED UP WITH RULES
AND THE ROOMFUL OF FOOLS
AT MY OFFICE WAS DRIVING ME NUTS.
WELL I NEEDED SOME PEACE
OR AT LEAST A RELEASE
OR I'D KICK IN THEIR IFS, ANDS, AND BUTTS.
BUT AT FIVE I PUNCH THE CLOCK AND NOT MY BOSS
AND I RUN HOME TO BECOME DIANA ROSS.
  All.
I JOINED AN ALL-GIRL BAND
AND THE FEELING IS JUST WHAT I NEED.
I JOINED AN ALL-GIRL BAND.

THIRD ACTRESS.
FROM NOW ON I'M SINGING THE LEAD!

(*FOURTH and FIFTH ACTRESSES enter from* DS. L. *and* R.,
respectively.)

ALL.
WE'RE SHAKIN' OUR MARACAS.
WE'RE MAKING NEWS,
MAKING MUSIC THAT'S RHYTHM AND BLUES.
TOGETHER WE'RE MUCH BETTER THAN SO-SO—
EACH OF US IS A VIRTUOSO!
FOURTH ACTRESS.
I WAS HITTIN' THE SKIDS.
FIFTH ACTRESS.
I WAS SICK OF MY KIDS.
FOURTH and FIFTH ACTRESSES.
DISCONTENTED TO JUST BE A WIFE.
FIFTH ACTRESS.
IF I SPENT ONE MORE DAY
WITH THE DAMN P.T.A.,
I WOULD DROWN IN THE CAR-POOL OF LIFE.
FOURTH ACTRESS.
THEN WE GAVE UP PLAYING
MAH JONG,
BRIDGE
FIFTH ACTRESS.
AND GIN.
FOURTH ACTRESS.
NOW I PLAY THE BASS GUITAR.
FIFTH ACTRESS.
AND VIOLIN.
ALL.
WE JOINED AN ALL-GIRL BAND
AND THE MUSIC INSIDE OF US SINGS.
WE JOINED AN ALL-GIRL BAND,
NOW LOOK WHOSE PULLING THE STRINGS!

WE JOINED AN ALL-GIRL BAND,
AND THE HARMONY SOARS THROUGH THE NIGHT.
WE JOINED AN ALL-GIRL BAND
ALICE IS DOING ALL RIGHT!

ALICE POEMS

(*spoken with piano under*)

FIFTH ACTRESS.
A . . . my name is Alice
And my husband's name is Allan
And we live in Alabama
And we sell apples.
FOURTH ACTRESS.
A . . . my name is Alice
And my husband's name is Albert
And I live in Albuquerque
And I get alimony.
THIRD ACTRESS.
A . . . my name is Alice
And I work as an attorney
For Applebaum, Bemshick and Cohen
And do I have anxiety!
SECOND ACTRESS.
A . . . my name is Alice
And I live in an apartment
And I live in it alone
And it's kind of antiseptic
And my boyfriend's an accountant
And he's kind of antisocial
And I wanted to be an actress
But I couldn't get an agent
So I sell Avon.
(*Chime does "ding-dong."*)
FIRST ACTRESS.
A . . . my name is Alice
And my husband's name is Adam
And his girlfriend's name is Amy
And my lover's name is Abbie
And her husband's name is Arnie
And his boyfriend's name is Allen
And my analyst's name is Arthur
And we're working on my anger

ALL-GIRL BAND TAG

ALL. (*singing*)
WE JOINED AN ALL-GIRL BAND

AND THE HARMONY SOARS THROUGH THE NIGHT.
WE JOINED AN ALL-GIRL BAND.
   FIRST and SECOND ACTRESSES.
NOW I CAN BLOW MY OWN HORN.
   THIRD ACTRESS.
FROM NOW ON I'M SINGING THE LEAD.
   FOURTH and FIFTH ACTRESSES.
NOW LOOK WHO'S PULLING THE STRINGS.
   ALL.
ALICE IS DOING ALL RIGHT!
(*Blackout*)

AT MY AGE

Lights come up to discover VICKY standing by a chair stage
   L., *primping. Throughout the song, she and KAREN play*
   to imaginary mirrors, miming different motions such as
   combing hair, putting on mascara, and lipstick, etc.

   VICKY.
THIRTY-TWO YEARS YOU LIVE WITH A MAN
AND YOU LOSE HIM.
THERE YOU ARE
WITH HIS PICTURE AND A HOUSEFUL OF MEMORIES.
   KAREN. (*enters and stands right of* C. *stage, primping*)
FIFTEEN YEARS OLD
AND I'VE NEVER EVEN GONE STEADY.
ALL MY GIRLFRIENDS
THINK IT'S KIND OF WEIRD.
   VICKY.
DIDN'T WANT TO START AGAIN.
   KAREN.
COULDN'T WAIT TO START.
HE'S SO GORGEOUS
AND HE'S GOING OUT FOR TRACK.
   VICKY.
OUT OF THE BLUE AUNT SARAH CALLED.
"I'VE GOT SOMEONE FOR YOU.
WALTER'S DEAD—
SITTING HOME WON'T BRING HIM BACK."
AND IT'S MY FIRST BLIND DATE . . .
   KAREN.
MY FIRST REAL DATE . . .

VICKY.
AT MY AGE.
KAREN.
AT MY AGE.
VICKY.
I'M NOT READY.
KAREN.
I'VE BEEN READY FOR SO LONG.
VICKY.
WHAT'LL WE DO FOR A WHOLE LONG EVENING?
WHAT DO YOU SAY TO A PERFECT STRANGER?
KAREN.
WHY DOES THIS KINKY HAIRCUT LOOK ALL WRONG?
WONDER IF MOM'S CHANEL SMELLS TOO STRONG?
HOW COULD I KNOW THAT MY BROTHER
WOULD GET HIM TO CALL ME?
THEN HE PHONED
AND I COULDN'T GET MY VOICE TO COOPERATE . . .
VICKY.
FIFTEEN YEARS OLD
IS WHAT I SUDDENLY FEEL LIKE —
CLAMMY HANDS
AND THAT LONG-FORGOTTEN ACHE.
KAREN.
PARALYZED AND TERRIFIED.
VICKY.
NOT A THING TO WEAR . . .
HE'S FROM SCARSDALE.
KAREN.
SHOULD I TRY TO SMOKE?
MAYBE HE'LL GET HIS FATHER'S CAR.
VICKY.
HE'S FIFTY-EIGHT YEARS OLD
AND A BROKER —
SO HE'LL PROBABLY GO FOR BROKE.
AND IT'S MY FIRST BLIND DATE . . .
KAREN.
MY FIRST REAL DATE —
IT'S CRAZY!
VICKY.
IT'S CRAZY!
KAREN.
WILL HE LIKE ME?

BOTH.
WILL HELLO BE JUST GOOD-BYE?
VICKY.
WHAT'LL I DO IF HE WANTS TO KISS ME?
KAREN.
WHAT'LL I DO IF HE TRIES TO FRENCH ME?
VICKY.
KISSING IS NOT THE PROBLEM.
KAREN.
I MAY DIE!
BOTH.
WHAT'LL I DO IF HE DOESN'T EVEN TRY?
IT'S ALL SO NEW—
IT'S A FIRST ALL RIGHT!
KAREN.
LIKE ALGEBRA OR CHAUCER.
VICKY.
LIKE THAT FIRST NIGHT.
BOTH.
AND HERE I AM—ANOTHER FIRST.
WELL, IT WON'T BE THE LAST,
BUT IT MAY BE THE WORST!
KAREN.
MY FIRST REAL DATE.
VICKY.
MY FIRST BLIND DATE.
KAREN.
WHO'S NERVOUS?
VICKY.
WHO'S NERVOUS?
BOTH.
I HOPE I DON'T START ACTING LIKE A FOOL.
KAREN.
MY FIRST REAL DATE . . .
VICKY.
MY FIRST BLIND DATE . . .
KAREN.
AT MY AGE.
VICKY.
AT MY AGE.
KAREN.
HE'LL THINK I'M A WIMP.

VICKY.
OLD FASHIONED OR ODD.
  KAREN.
MY I.D.!
  VICKY.
MY NEW BAG!
  BOTH.
HE'S HERE! OH, MY GOD!
BE COOL. . . .
(*Both stand and take a few steps* DS.)
(*spoken*) Hello.
(*Blackout*)

TRASH

Lights come up to discover MINDY sitting stage L., *reading a*
  paperback novel. A desk is set DS.R.

VOICE-OVER. "Jacqueline: she had the kind of beauty that
made men burn with desire. She was every woman's envy and
every man's dream. Yet she was possessed by a lover whose
cruelty was ravishing torment." (*MINDY puts down the first
novel and picks up a second from the table beside her.*) "Babette:
the world was her bedroom. From the beaches of St. Tropez to
the boardrooms of Manhattan's super-rich; from the back-
streets of Florence to the pyramids of Cairo; from the casinos of
Las Vegas to the jungles of Peru. Babette: she was a woman who
couldn't stay put." (*MINDY puts down the paperback.*)
  MINDY. Mindy: she had everything. An exciting job as a receptionist for a woman's shoe manufacturer, a studio apartment
in Queens, a boyfriend of limited qualities, and yet somehow she
knew, there had to be more. (*As the song intro begins she stands
and crosses to* C. *stage. Singing:*)
SHE DRESSED AND TOOK THE DOUBLE R,
AND PRESSED INSIDE THE CROWDED CAR,
REGRETTED HAVING LEFT THE LIMOUSINE AT HOME.
SHE HID BEHIND HER DAILY NEWS
AND WONDERED WHAT HAD MADE HER CHOOSE
THIS CRAZY LIFE OF DANGER, SEX AND BOOZE
AT KAPLAN'S SHOES.

SHE FOUND HER OFFICE DOOR UNLOCKED—

SHE HELD HER BREATH AND GENTLY KNOCKED.
SHE HEARD A SOUND AND HID BEHIND HER DESK.

(*MRS. KAPLAN enters.*)

HER RIVAL ENTERED DRESSED IN RED,
AND MINDY SWORE SHE'D SEE HER DEAD.
SHE GRABBED THE ROLODEX AND RAISED IT,
BUT INSTEAD THE WOMAN SAID:
    MRS. KAPLAN. (*speaking*) Mindy, type this up for me, and I'll
need three copies. (*sees Rolodex over MINDY's head*) Oh, and
can you get me Milton Glaser's phone number. (*MRS.
KAPLAN exits.*)
    MINDY. (*singing*)
WHY CAN'T MY LIFE BE TRASH?
WHY CAN'T I WAKE UP TO SCORCHING ROMANCE?
TORN FROM THE PAGES OF COLLINS OR KRANTZ?
OH, WHY CAN'T MY LIFE BE TRASH?

(*HOWARD enters* US.C. *and crosses to MINDY.*)

    MINDY. (*continued*)
THEN HOWARD RUSHED INTO THE ROOM,
AND MINDY SENSED IMPENDING DOOM
HE SLIPPED AN INVOICE IN HER IN-BOX AND HE
    SMILED.
    HOWARD. (*speaking*) Hi, Mindy. (*HOWARD flexes his
biceps as he sings.*)
SHE MARVELED AT HIS FINE PHYSIQUE,
HIS BULGING PECKS THAT LEFT HER WEAK.
SHE WATCHED HIM FLEX
WITH THOUGHTS OF SEX
AND MINDY TRIED TO SPEAK.
SHE TOUCHED HIS CHEEK.
(*They talk as the music continues.*)
    MINDY. (*touches his cheek*) You have something here, How-
ard.
    HOWARD. Oh. Tuna salad. Listen, Mindy. I've been thinking
. . . . I think maybe we should start seeing other people. I mean
we work in the same office and all and we've been seeing each
other for three years now, and I dunno. . . .
    MINDY. (*singing, as she pushes HOWARD offstage*)

WHY CAN'T HE TREAT ME LIKE TRASH?
(*speaking*) We'll talk about it later, Howard. (*singing*)
WHY CAN'T HE PULL ME TO STRONG SPANISH HIPS?
TAKE ME AND TEAR OUT MY HEART WITH HIS LIPS?
UNLEASH ALL I'VE HELD IN ME?
COMPLETELY SIDNEY SHELDON ME??

(*STANLEY enters, carrying a briefcase. He has a trucking walk and a snappy style.*)

MINDY. May I help you?

STANLEY. Stanley Henderson. I have an appointment with Mrs. Kaplan. Leather samples. (*indicates briefcase*)

MINDY. Have a seat. (*sees thick paperback book that STAN-LEY has pulled out and is reading*) Oh, I've been meaning to read that—how is it?

STANLEY. Pretty good. I liked *Forbidden Tears* a lot better.

MINDY. (*into intercom*) Mrs. K, your ten o'clock appointment is here.

STANLEY. (*to himself*) From the moment he laid eyes on her he knew he had to possess her.

MINDY. Pardon?

STANLEY. Nothing. He knew that behind that icy exterior lived a hot-blooded siren, sensuous and exotic. (*MINDY has mean-while taken a stick of gum from her desk and has slunk to the other side of STANLEY.*)

MINDY. Gum? (*STANLEY shakes his head.*) Her heart was pounding. She looked at him again and raw passion welled within her.

STANLEY. He met her gaze, and his eyes danced with cruel amusement. (*His eyes do so.*)

MINDY. She had to turn away. . . . How does he do that? (*She mimics STANLEY's eyes.*)

STANLEY. He approached her slowly, and touched her arm. (*He crosses to MINDY.*)

MINDY. Sending shivers up her spine.

STANLEY. He held her close. (*MINDY is wrapped in STAN-LEY's arms. They sing romantic nothings to each other.*)

STANLEY.
AAAHHH . . .

MINDY.
AAAHHH . . .

STANLEY.
AAAHHH . . .
MINDY.
AAAHHH . . .
STANLEY.
AAAHHH . . .
MINDY.
AAAHHH . . .

MINDY. Mindy closed her eyes, secure at last in the strength of his firm embrace.

STANLEY. But of course theirs was a love that was never meant to be.

MINDY. (*puzzled*) Oh, yeah? Why's that?

STANLEY. Because of the secret pact they had made years before aboard the Baron's yacht.

MINDY. (*thinking fast*) Ah, the Baron's yacht, yes, but . . . but she was suffering from amnesia then and has only recently begun to piece together the puzzle of her former life.

STANLEY. Perhaps. Then of course she remembers that she was a lady of the evening then, and he a simple priest. (*He assumes priestly pose.*)

MINDY. (*desperate now*) But things have changed! Now she's a world famous fashion model! (*She poses.*)

STANLEY. And he's the Pope!

MINDY. Oh. (*The intercom buzzes and the fantasy is over.*) Mrs. Kaplan will see you now. (*STANLEY prepares to leave.*) We always have tomorrow. (*She drapes herself on the desk.*)

STANLEY. I already read it. It's not very good. (*He exits. MINDY returns to her desk and sits dejectedly.*)

MINDY. Broken and defeated, Mindy sat down at her desk. She filed some invoices, wrote out a disbursement, sharpened a pencil . . . (*singing*)
WHY CAN'T MY LIFE BE . . .
(*Inspiration hits. She presses the intercom button. Speaking—*)
Howard, it's Mindy. Can you come in here? I got a book I want you to read.
(*Blackout*)

FOR WOMEN ONLY #1

A single spot comes up c. stage as a POETESS enters, carrying a huge elaborately covered book.

POETESS. A poem. From my collection, *For Women Only.*
(*She recites.*)
I am woman.
A crippled bird.
The ledge is cold,
My wings are clipped.
He did it.
He did it.
I was his pretty Polly.
Pity Polly.
Pity pretty Polly
Doesn't want a cracker.
I am woman.
A crippled bird.
F — flap
(*The light starts to fade.*)
F — flap
F — flap
F —
(*The light is out.*)

GOOD THING I LEARNED TO DANCE

The lights come up as an ACTRESS enters and tap dances at
c. *stage. She sings.*

ACTRESS.
LITTLE GIRLS CANNOT RESIST A TAP CLASS.
LITTLE GIRLS BY SIX CAN KEEP A BEAT.
I DON'T THINK I EVER MISSED A TAP CLASS.
WHO'D'VE GUESSED WHAT SOUNDS COULD COME
    FROM FEET?

GOOD THING I LEARNED TO DANCE.
GOOD THING I LEARNED TO DANCE.
LITTLE GIRLS ARE NOT SUPPOSED TO SHOUT,
SO I STAYED WELL-BEHAVED.
I KEPT MY BAD SELF SAVED
FOR TWICE A WEEK WHEN I COULD LET IT OUT.

(*Her MOTHER's voice is heard from offstage. After each
    admonishment, the girl reacts with a tap pattern.*)

MOTHER. (*speaking*) Now, don't be showing off in front of your friends, acting fast. (*She taps.*) You just tap dance yourself into that kitchen and do those dishes! (*She taps.*) I'm gonna do a tap dance upside your head if you don't get into bed! (*She taps violently. The girl ages to early adolescence.*)

ACTRESS. (*singing*)
TEEN-AGE GIRLS LOVE JUNIOR HIGH SCHOOL SOCIALS.
LOTS OF TIMES WE WENT WITHOUT A DATE.
TEEN-AGE BOYS WERE SHY AT MY SCHOOL SOCIALS.
I WAS GONNA SIT AROUND AND WAIT? UH-UH!

GOOD THING I LEARNED TO DANCE.
GOOD THING I LEARNED TO DANCE.
TWO BY TWO THE GIRLS WOULD START TO SHAKE.
THE BOYS WOULD STAND AND STARE.
WE'D BE TOO COOL TO CARE,
WHILE THEY FIGURED OUT WHAT MOVE TO MAKE.
(*speaking while dancing with invisible partner*) You like this move, Clara? It's called the Four Corners. They're trying to get this on "Shindig." When Mary Alice does it, she goes all up in the air. (*demonstrates*) If that doesn't get those boys across the gym, they are dead . . . Oh, Clara, they *are* dead! (*She checks out crowd.*) Ohhh, look at Joyce Webb, dancing by herself. Y'know, it's true about Joyce. I'm in her gym class and I saw for myself. She sent away for these pills to enlarge her breasts, and you know what happened? Her nipples disappeared! (*She ages again, and is now a contemporary woman. Singing—*)
GROWN UP WOMEN HURRY TO THE CITY.
I HAD NOTHING LEFT BUT DREAMS TO LOSE.
AIMLESSLY I WANDERED THROUGH THE CITY,
DANCED AT NIGHT TO KICK AWAY MY BLUES.

GOOD THING I LEARNED TO DANCE.
GOOD THING I LEARNED TO DANCE.
LATE ONE NIGHT A STRANGER CAME MY WAY.
HE FLASHED HIS CARD AND SMILE.
HE SAID "YOU MOVE WITH STYLE,"
AND THAT'S HOW I GOT WHERE I AM TODAY!

(*She doffs, her skirt to reveal an exercise leotard. She exercises throughout. Speaking—*)

And stretch and breathe,
and stretch and breathe.
Welcome ladies, to the Beverly Hills branch
of Boogie for Beauty.

And one, and two . . .

Come on ladies, if you want to slim up, you got to get down.
If you want to remove it, you got to groove it!
You've got to rock to lose those rolls!

(*She sings.*)
GOOD THING I LEARNED TO DANCE.
GOOD THING I LEARNED TO DANCE.
GOOD THING I LEARNED . . .
IT'S A GOOD THING I LEARNED TO DANCE!
(*Blackout*)

WELCOME TO KINDERGARTEN, MRS. JOHNSON

Lights up on simple schoolroom set. MS. THOMAS is at her desk, stage L. She is wearing a bright smock. As MRS. JOHNSON enters, MS. THOMAS crosses to her.

Ms. THOMAS. Welcome to kindergarten, Mrs. Johnson.
MRS. JOHNSON. How do you do? It's a pleasure meeting you. Janie has told me so much about you.
Ms. THOMAS. It's a shame you couldn't make it last week with the other mothers.
MRS. JOHNSON. I'm sorry. I was speaking at a conference in Zurich.
Ms. THOMAS. Well, come along. (*crosses back to her desk*) I've been observing Janie very closely. Have a seat. (*MRS. JOHNSON starts to sit in a miniature kiddy chair and nearly falls off onto the floor. MS. THOMAS, oblivious to her difficulty.*) Sit up straight. (*She sings.*)
SHE'S A VERY BRIGHT GIRL, MRS. JOHNSON.
SHE WORKS BEYOND POTENTIAL —
A MODEL FOR HER PEERS,
EXPLORING AT A LEVEL
THAT IS WAY BEYOND HER YEARS.

AND I'M SORRY
BUT IT'S GETTING ON MY NERVES.
    Mrs. Johnson. (*speaking*) I'm sorry. . . .
    Ms. Thomas. (*speaking*) Don't fidget, Mrs. Johnson. (*crosses to MRS. JOHNSON, singing*)
SHE'S A DIFFICULT GIRL, MRS. JOHNSON.
SHE HELPS THE OTHER CHILDREN—LORD KNOWS
    WHERE IT WILL LEAD,
AND I'VE LEARNED THAT WHEN MY BACK IS TURNED
SHE'S TEACHING THEM TO READ.
I'M TO SAY THE LEAST DISMAYED—,
WHAT DOES SHE THINK THIS IS, THIRD GRADE?

SHE'S INDEPENDENT.
SHE'S ASSERTIVE.
SHE'S ALWAYS SELF-ASSURED.
NOW I DON'T KNOW WHERE SHE'S GETTING THAT,
BUT IT'S NOT TO BE IGNORED—
AND IT GENERALLY STARTS AT THE HOME.

(*MS. THOMAS sits back at her desk. Speaking—*) Did you know that Janie's the only child in class with an even reasonable self-image? Now who's responsible for *that*?
    Mrs. Johnson. (*a bit thrown*) I am.
    Ms. Thomas. I'm sorry?
    Mrs. Johnson. (*louder*) I am.
    Ms. Thomas. I am *what*?
    Mrs. Johnson. I am, Ms. Thomas.
    Ms. Thomas. Good. Well, how do you expect her to be intimidated by simple authority?
    Mrs. Johnson. Well, I . . . (*starts to sit on her hands*)
    Ms. Thomas. Keep your hands where I can see them. (*MRS. JOHNSON jerks her hands up. MS. THOMAS sings.*)
NOW, I'M NOT SAYING YOU'RE A BAD MOTHER,
EVEN THOUGH YOU MISSED OUR PAGEANT
AND THE HALLOWEEN PARADE.
NO, NO ONE'S SAYING YOU'RE A
(*produces Bad Mother flash card*)

BAD MOTHER,
BUT YOUR COOKIES AT THE BAKE SALE,
WELL, THEY CLEARLY WEREN'T HOMEMADE.

MRS. JOHNSON. (*abashed; speaking —*) They were Pepperidge Farm Mint Milanos.

Ms. THOMAS. The other mothers baked.

MRS. JOHNSON. I know, but . . . but I hate baking.

Ms. THOMAS. Janie was humiliated!

MRS. JOHNSON. She never said a thing to me!

Ms. THOMAS. Well . . . (*singing*)
YOU'RE A BUSY LITTLE BEE, MRS. JOHNSON,
ZIPPING OFF TO ZURICH.
I HEAR NEXT WEEK IT'S ROME.
IS THERE REALLY ANY WONDER
THINGS ARE SUFFERING AT HOME?
(*MRS. JOHNSON starts to protest.*)

OH, THERE'S NO NEED TO OBJECT.
IT'S ALL HERE IN JANIE'S ARTWORK —
YOU CAN SEE THAT I'M CORRECT.
(*She produces a large pig made out of a Clorox bottle and decorated with hearts. She shows it to MRS. JOHNSON.*)

MRS. JOHNSON. (*speaking*) It's a pig! Made out of a Clorox bottle!

Ms. THOMAS. Oh, come on, Mrs. Johnson. There are domestic problems written all over this pig. I know what I'm talking about. I've taken psychology courses.

MRS. JOHNSON. (*starting to stand*) But . . .

Ms. THOMAS. (*raising pig over MRS. JOHNSON's head*) If you have something to say you raise your hand! (*MRS. JOHNSON sits abruptly, MS. THOMAS sings:*)
NOW, NO ONE WANTS TO BE A —
(*MS. THOMAS flashes card at MRS. JOHNSON.*)

MRS. JOHNSON.
BAD MOTHER.

Ms. THOMAS.
AND I THINK WE CAN DO BETTER
IF WE JUST MAKE UP OUR MINDS,
'CAUSE WE ALL KNOW WHAT HAPPENS TO A —
(*She flashes card again at MRS. JOHNSON.*)

MRS. JOHNSON.
BAD MOTHER!

Ms. THOMAS.
MS. THOMAS:
AND THERE'S EVERY INDICATION

THAT THIS SUITS YOUR SITUATION.
HERE IS MY EVALUATION—
TAKE IT HOME AND HAVE IT SIGNED!
(*She picks up an evaluation with 'Bad Mother' marked on it and pins it on MRS. JOHNSON, who is crushed.*)
(*speaking*) Now, wasn't it nice meeting and getting a chance to chat like this?

    Mrs. Johnson. (*fighting back tears*) Uh-huh.

    Ms. Thomas. Did you know we have these parent-teacher conferences every Monday at four o'clock?

    Mrs. Johnson. (*shaking head*) Un-uh.

    Ms. Thomas. Well, I hope I'll be seeing you again very soon. (*She replaces the pig.*)

    Mrs. Johnson. Ye-yes, Ms. Thomas.

    Ms. Thomas. That'll be all. (*MRS. JOHNSON tears out of the classroom.*) No running in the halls. (*She sees the next mother waiting.*) Welcome to kindergarten, Mrs. Feldman. Have a seat.

(*Blackout*)

I SURE LIKE THE BOYS

Lights discover an ACTRESS stage r. The song is lyrical, full of the innocent sensuality of a young woman discovering sex.

I SURE LIKE THE BOYS WHO LIKE TO DANCE REAL
    SLOW.
WHERE THEY LEAD IS WHERE I GO.
DIP ME DOWN, SPIN ME ROUND,
WE'LL MAKE HISTORY IN THIS LITTLE TOWN.
I SURE LIKE THE BOYS WHO LIKE TO DANCE REAL
    SLOW.
(*crosses slowly to stage l.*)

I SURE LIKE THE BOYS WHO LIKE TO DRIVE REAL
    SLOW.
NO RUSH, YOU KNOW WE'LL GET THERE.
PARKING BY THE LAKESIDE,
HEADLIGHTS IN THE MOONLIGHT—
ONE LOOK AT ME AND OFF THEY GO.

KISS ME REAL SLOW.

NO RUSH, YOU KNOW.
FEEL EVERY CORNER,
TRY EVERY SPOT—
HERE ARE MY LIPS, MY HAIR, MY EYES, MY HEART.
I SURE LIKE THE BOYS
WHO LIKE TO DANCE REAL SLOW.
(*crosses slowly to* C. *stage*)

I SURE LIKE THE BOYS WHO LIKE TO HUM REAL SLOW
TO THE LOVE SONGS WE LOVE ON THE RADIO.
TOO SHY TO SAY "DON'T EVER GO"
AND TOO SHY TO SAY "I LOVE YOU SO"—
BUT HUMMING ALONG AND LETTING ME KNOW.

(*hums first two lines of chorus*)
FEEL EVERY CORNER,
TRY EVERY SPOT—
HERE ARE MY LIPS, MY HAIR, MY EYES, MY HEART.
I SURE LIKE THE BOYS WHO LIKE TO DANCE REAL
    SLOW.
(*Blackout*)

MS. MAE

Lights up as MS. MAE enters DS.L. *and crosses to three chairs set up to resemble a beauty parlor chair. She is wearing a barber's bib and a towel around her neck and is carrying a handbag. She is very old and moves slowly. She plays as if there is a mirror* DS. *of the chair, with unseen beautician standing behind her.*

MRS. MAE. Ohh! Girl! You washed that out real, real nice, didn't ya! Just as shiny and pretty! I like that! Child, you just tell me where to sit now. You just tell me how you want me. This way? Well, okay, all right now. (*Her head suddenly snaps backwards as the beautician starts to comb her hair. This continues for a time.*) Child, just rake that brush through them naps now! I'm not tender-headed. . . . Give them burrs a whippin'! Naw, naw it don't hurt me none—the pain feels good! (*She pats her face with a Kleenex. The brushing resumes.*) You see this here is the first time I ever had to set foot inside anybody's beauty parlor since I don't know when. Since near about half a century. I'm used to doing my own naps myself, but since the arthu-ri-tis done and seeped down into my knitting thumb so bad . . . (*She turns around while speaking to look directly at the beautician.*) Oh, turn around? I'm sorry. . . . I'm seventy-two going on seventy-three! (*The direction of the brushing changes, so her head is now going forward.*) Tell you something my grandmammy used to tell me. "A woman's head of hair is her crowning glory." Yes ma'am, that's what we was brought up to believe and that's what I hold to to this day. Say what? (*The brushing ends and MS. MAE feels the back of her head.*) There's a patch back there not dry yet. Naw, naw, I don't have to get back under the drier for that. (*She crosses to a small table and picks up a magazine and a fan. She returns to her chair and fans herself periodically throughout the rest of the monologue.*) Go ahead and heat up the comb. Leave it to simmer on the grill a little bit more. Make sure the metal tips of the comb glow red, red hot. That's the onliest way to do me a good press. Wigs! No, I don't like them wigs and fake braids strung down the back or those corn-rows with the ringlets and the what not, like you see so many of the people walking around today—trying to make believe they're Polynesian royalty. (*laughs*) Like this gal I seen coming home out the train the other night. Let's see, was it Wednesday? Yes, it was Wednesday, cause Wednesday's my choir practice night and . . . Oh, Mt. Zion, yes that's right, right there on Convent Avenue, that's the one. Oh, Ebenezer Baptist? Why yes, I know your church. That was Reverend Gaines's old church before he passed, bless his heart. Yes, I heard about it. Fell right out of the pulpit, didn't he? Well, you never know, when your time is up, when the call comes, you just got to go. That's right, amen! . . . Now let me tell you about this gal. Honey, she was fine. One of our peoples, fine as wine. Had on real sharp clothes for days, hair all coiffed real fluffy, all these long pretty curls down her back. She was one of them long-leggedy gals. Had her hemline jacked up to there so she could show off them shapely hams. (*MS. MAE demonstrates.*) She would crisscross them this way, then crisscross them that way. Then she commenced to a-tossing and a-flinging, and a-flinging and a-tossing. Child just sending up smoke signals something awful. Had all the men folk skittish. Yes she did! Well, anyway, we're ridin' along on the train, and we stopped at Fifty-ninth Street and the door flew open. Peoples comin' and goin', and in walked this nobody character. You know—one of them faceless folk you don't pay too much attention to. Well, anyway, this Mr. Faceless had his stuff timed out precise and on the button, because before you could blink twice this shadow-of-a-lowlife had done jumped up, snatched off the woman's hair, leaped out the door and the train took off! Yessir! If I'm lying I'm flying! There she sat with her whole head nekked! I just can't describe it — but let me tell you! She was the most pitiful sight! Little teeny piggy twigs all over her nappy head. Her real live hair wasn't as long as a baby maggot. You know those teeny stubbles with the twisted knots so short they don't have tips? Yes, "buckwheat bubbles"! That's what we used to call 'em. And you know she was humiliated, 'cause it's a long haul from Fifty-ninth Street to One Hundred Twenty-Fifth before she could jump off and hide herself. And to top it all off, wouldn't you know that this would be the one car in the whole entire train just brimmin' over with all God's white folk in creation, all goin' uptown — I don't know where — past Harlem. And why they had to choose this car on this particular night with this child shamed low, I'll never know. I felt so put out with her sittin' up there in the open lookin' like that. And here them white folk ain't hardly got used to seein' us in the rough, much less knowin' what to make of this chile sittin' up there lookin' like a burr-headed pickaninny from off the plantation! And the few colored peoples there was, they're dippin' their heads down into their necks tryin' to look off and away, and then the white folk tryin' to look into their faces to see how they're supposed to react. Child, it was all too embarrassing. I just wanted to reach into my handbag to seek out a scarf or hankie to help the poor thing out of her misery, like any good Christian woman should . . but then, I didn't know the girl . . . I thought she might feel worse, get the wrong idea That's why I tell my grands, and my great-grands and my nieces and all of me and mine that that's what you get for totin' somethin' fake. Wear your real hair and go about your business. Don't cop no stick-up attitude, no false pride, 'cause the Lord will lay you low, yes he will! Hallelujah! (*She once more becomes aware of herself in the mirror.*) Oh, my, this is turning out real fine. I like that, I like that. I can see where I'm gonna be comin' from now on. Come on around here where I can see you. (*She motions beautician around.*) Now, you must stop by Mt. Zion Church one of these Sundays. (*Lights start to fade as gospel music begins under.*) In fact, let me have your address, cause we're having a church raffle for our building fund and I'll send you a stub for you and your husband. . . . (*Lights are out.*)

DETROIT PERSONS

*Lights come up as the DETROIT PERSONS burst in from
the various entrances, bouncing basketballs and performing
tricks with them. Sport show music plays underneath.
ROSIE CASSIDY, an older woman, tries to quiet them
down as showtime approaches.*

ROSIE. All right, ladies . . . five seconds to air time . . .
three . . . two . . . one . . . Hi Sports! Rosie Cassidy here!
Welcome to the ZBS Cavalcade of Sports. Tonight I have here
with me America's foremost female exhibition basketball team,
the Detroit Persons. The Persons have been kind enough to take
a few moments off from their whirlwind cross-country tour to
share some of their intimate thoughts with us. Now, I notice
there are only four of you here today. Where is your star forward, Nadine Johnson?
SHERIDAN GRACE. (*crosses to ROSIE*) Oh, Nadine . . . she's
doin' a thing for coke.
ROSIE. (*misunderstanding*) How wonderful . . . a commer-
cial.
SHERIDAN. Uh-uh honey. This ain't no endorsement. She doin'
time for coke. (*crosses away*)
ROSIE. Aha. (*crosses to VONELLE*) So ladies, tell me . . .
(*She places her hand companionably on VONELLE's shoulder.
VONELLE turns her head and glares at ROSIE's hand.*) As an
exhibition team . . . (*sees the glare and snatches her hand away*)
Right . . . as an exhibition team, you're on the road an average
of two weeks every month. How does this affect you personally?
VONELLE. Bricks get laid more than me, Rosie.
SHERIDAN. Yo, Spike here has it good. Her husband travels
with her.
ROSIE. (*crosses to SPIKE*) Spike Martin. What a well-rounded
person you are. I understand that along with a husband and two
children, you have also managed to obtain a master's degree in
English literature from Yale.
SPIKE. That's right, Rosie. See, for me it was a toss-up between seventeenth-century metaphysical poetry and sports.
ROSIE. Well, how did you come to choose the sports over the
poetry?
SPIKE. I started to go for my PhD., but my mind kept return-
ing to athletics. I missed the feeling I used to get when I stole

bases as a kid. You know, the thrill of sliding in there with my spikes flying . . . (*She begins to build in intensity as ROSIE gestures to the off-camera director to cut.*) The elation of sinking my metal cleats into the vulnerable flesh of my opponent. The high I got when the ruby red blood began to gush out of the veins, when the face contorted into a horrible mask of excruciating pain, when the helpless body writhed on the ground in spasms of anguished nausea, when . . . (*SPIKE rips open her jacket to reveal spiked leather bands.*)

ROSIE. (*desperate*) Hence, the name "Spike."

SPIKE. Hence. (*VONELLE dribbles her ball down to ROSIE.*)

ROSIE. Vonelle Grace, I understand you made a tremendous comeback from injuries to play basketball this year.

VONELLE. That's right, Rosie. My whole body like to give out on me.

ROSIE. But now you are in tip-top shape. What gave you the will to go on? (*SHERIDAN has been quietly moving to directly us. of ROSIE.*)

VONELLE. Well, I'd have to give credit to my sister Sheridan here. (*They slap hands loudly just behind ROSIE's head, startling her.*) Whenever I got real down, she'd say to me, "Honey, just pick yourself up, go out there on the court, and hurt somebody." (*She pitches her basketball into ROSIE's stomach.*)

ROSIE. (*doubled over in pain*) Thank you, Vonelle. You're an inspiration to us all. (*She sees the next player approaching.*) Wanda Handwerger, you've been playing professional basketball in this country for over seven years. . . .

SHERIDAN. And she still don't speak so good English neither . . . (*WANDA glares.*)

ROSIE. Do you feel there are any significant differences between men's and women's basketball?

WANDA. (*in a heavy accent*) Say again, please?

ROSIE. (*very slowly*) Do you see any differences in men and women basketball players?

WANDA. Ah! Our cycle. They do not have.

ROSIE. I beg your pardon?

WANDA. My voman's body. One or two days a month I find myself to cry out at the referee for every close call. I veep when I miss the yump shot. I am very cross with my boyfriend. Male players do not have this, I think. (*She clicks her tongue.*)

ROSIE. Thank you, Wanda. Now I understand you have planned a special demonstration for us today. Is that right?

WANDA. Oh, yes, by golly. We want to expose ourselves on national tee wee.

SPIKE. Exposure, Wanda, we want exposure.

(*The players pile their basketballs on ROSIE, who exits as they break into a spirited dance that incorporates basketball tricks. They sing.*)

EDUCATED FEET

SHERIDAN.
WE GOT HUSTLE,
WE GOT HEAT.
OTHERS.
WE GOT HUSTLE,
WE GOT HEAT.
SHERIDAN.
LEARNED OUR FIGHTIN'
ON THE STREET.
OTHERS.
DIRTY FIGHTIN'
ON THE STREET.
SHERIDAN.
AND TO MAKE IT REAL COMPLETE —
ALL.
WE LOOK GOOD ENOUGH TO EAT.
WE GOT ED-U-CA-TED FEET,
WE GOT EDUCATED FEET.
SPIKE.
WE GOT SPICE AND
WE GOT SPUNK.
OTHERS.
WE GOT SPICE AND
WE GOT SPUNK.
WANDA.
BOOGIE ON DOWN THE
COURT AND DUNK.
OTHERS.
BOOGIE ON DOWN THE
COURT AND DUNK.
VONELLE.
BOUNCE THE BALL AND SEE IT FLY.

ALL.
WATCH THE COMPETITION CRY.
WE GOT ED-U-CA-TED FEET.
WE GOT EDUCATED FEET.

WE'RE SAYIN' PH.D.
WE'RE SAYIN' M.B.A.
WE'RE SAYIN' VIC-TO-RY,
WE'RE SAYIN' HIP, HIP, HIP
HOORAY!

WE'RE GONNA GIVE YOU
SOMETHIN' SWEET.
GONNA GIVE'YOU
ATH-A-LETE.
WE GOT ED-U-CA-TED FEET,
WE GOT EDUCATED FEET.
    WANDA.
WE GOT WIM AND
WE GOT WERVE.
    ALL.
WE GOT VIM AND
WE GOT VERVE.
    WANDA.
WE GOT BRAINS AND
WE GOT NERVE.
    OTHERS.
WE GOT BRAINS AND
WE GOT NERVE.
    WANDA.
WE GOT MUSCLES WE CAN FLEX.
    ALL.
WE ARE NOT THE WEAKER SEX.
WE GOT ED-U-CA-TED FEET,
WE GOT EDUCATED FEET.

WE'RE SAYIN' PH.D.
WE'RE SAYIN' M.B.A.
WE'RE SAYIN' VIC-TO-RY,
WE'RE SAYIN' HIP, HIP, HIP
HOORAY!

WE'RE GONNA GIVE YOU
ATH-A-LETE.
WE GOT ED-U-CA-TED FEET.
WE GOT ED-U-CA-TED

(*speaking*) Feet, don't fail me now!
(*Blackout*)

FOR WOMEN ONLY #2

The POETESS enters US.C., *and crosses* DS. *slowly, once again lugging the book.*

POETESS. Another poem from my collection, *For Women Only.*
I am woman.
A neglected plant.
Hanging by the window
Waiting to be watered.
He did it.
He did it.
I was his philodendren
Calling out:
"Won't somebody talk
to me?"
I am woman.
A neglected plant.
D-droop
(*Lights begin to fade.*)
D-droop
D-droop
D—
(*Lights are out.*)

THE PORTRAIT

Lights come up to discover an ACTRESS sitting stage L. *She sings.*

THERE'S A PICTURE IN A SILVER FRAME
HANGING DUSTY ON MY WALL.
AND TWO PEOPLE WITH THEIR EYES THE SAME
HOLDING DAISIES, I RECALL.

AND THE BABY IN THE SAILOR DRESS
AND THE PIGTAILS — THAT WAS ME.
AND THE OTHER WAS MY MOTHER
ON OUR EASTER BY THE SEA.

PEOPLE TELL ME THAT I'M JUST LIKE HER,
AND I WONDER WHAT THEY SEE.
SHE WAS A LADY, LACE AND CAMEO,
NOT THE GYPSY THAT IS ME.
SHE SPENT HER EVENINGS MAKING POETRY.
I SPEND MY NIGHTS MAKING TIME.
AND WONDER, AM I LIVING?
PARTLY HER DREAMS, PARTLY MINE?

WHAT WOULD SHE THINK OF THE TOO MANY MEN,
THE LIES I GET LOST IN, AGAIN AND AGAIN,
THE TEARS IN THE MORNING, THE BOOZE
AND THE BLUES IN THE NIGHT.

IT'S BEEN YEARS NOW SINCE I'VE SEEN HER FACE,
HEARD HER FOOTSTEPS ON THE STAIR.
BUT JUST LATELY IN MY DREAMS AT NIGHT
I WILL CALL HER, AND SHE'S THERE,
LOOKING PRETTY, LIKE SHE USED TO,
BEFORE TIME AND TEARS TORE HER APART.
AND SHE TELLS ME THAT SHE LOVES ME,
THEN SHE LEAVES ME IN THE DARK.

MAMA DON'T LEAVE ME, MAMA DON'T GO
YOU KNOW THE ANSWERS TO ALL I DON'T KNOW.
(*stands, crosses to* c. *stage*)

MY DREAMS COME UP EMPTY AND MY HEART'S
LYING DEAD ON THE FLOOR.
MAMA DON'T LEAVE ME, MAMA PLEASE STAY.
MAMA I NEED YOU TO SHOW ME THE WAY.
I'M LOST AND I'M LONELY
AND I CAN'T FIND MY WAY ANYMORE —
MAMA,
MAMA.
(*The lights fade.*)

BLUER THAN YOU

Three ACTRESSES enter US.C. *Throughout the song, each tries to top the others in blueness.*

FIRST ACTRESS.
WHAT CAN I SAY? I GUESS THIS HASN'T BEEN MY
    DAY. . . .
SECOND ACTRESS.
WEEK . . .
THIRD ACTRESS.
DECADE.
SECOND ACTRESS.
I'M DISTURBED. . . .
FIRST ACTRESS.
I'M DISTRAUGHT. . . .
THIRD ACTRESS.
I'M DISTRESSED. . . . I'M OVERWROUGHT.
SECOND and THIRD ACTRESSES.
YOU'RE OVERDOING IT.
    ALL.
I'M UNHAPPY AND I DON'T KNOW WHY.
    FIRST ACTRESS.
I WOULD HAVE TO GET DOWN
TO GET HIGH.
    THIRD ACTRESS.
SO WOULD I.
    SECOND ACTRESS.
ME TOO!
    ALL.
I'M BLUE!
    FIRST ACTRESS.
MY MAN HE UP AND QUIT ME,
MY CLOTHES NO LONGER FIT ME
'CAUSE I'M STILL COOKIN' FOR TWO.
NO ONE WILL DATE ME.
EVEN GAY MEN SEEM TO HATE ME.
I'M BLUER THAN YOU.
    THIRD ACTRESS.
YOU THINK YOU'RE HURTIN', HONEY,
THE LAST TIME I MADE MONEY
WAS OCTOBER OF SEVENTY-THREE.

MY SHRINK'S ON THE EQUATOR,
DIAL-A-PRAYER SAID "CALL BACK LATER."
I'M BLUER THAN SHE!
SECOND ACTRESS.
OH, THE THINGS I'M SMOKIN'
SINCE I LOST MY FAVORITE BOY.
ALL MY NAILS ARE BROKEN,
SO WHAT'S LEFT TO ENJOY?
ALL.
OY!
FIRST ACTRESS.
I'M IN SUCH A QUANDRY.
SECOND ACTRESS.
I HAVEN'T DONE MY LAUNDRY.
THIRD ACTRESS.
I DON'T HAVE A LAUNDRY TO DO!
FIRST ACTRESS.
MY CO-OP'S GOING RENTAL.
SECOND ACTRESS.
AND MY HAIR'S TURNIN' GREY.
FIRST and THIRD ACTRESSES.
DAY BY DAY—
THIRD ACTRESS.
MY SATIN SHEETS ARE SHREDDING.
FIRST and SECOND ACTRESSES.
WE'RE INVITED TO A WEDDING.
ALL.
I'M BLUER THAN THEY . . . ARE
(*The following is spoken.*)
THIRD ACTRESS. Am I blue? Are these tears in my eyes telling you? . . .
SECOND ACTRESS. I mean . . . I mean my man calls me such terrible names.
FIRST ACTRESS. Your man speaks to you?
THIRD ACTRESS. (*trying to break in*) If I could just . . .
SECOND ACTRESS. I mean, I get up in the morning and I say, "Come right in heartache and have a seat."
FIRST ACTRESS. You can get up in the morning?
THIRD ACTRESS. Listen. . . .
SECOND ACTRESS. I got a right to sing the blues.
FIRST ACTRESS. Well, I know I got a right to sing the blues.
THIRD ACTRESS. Well, I don't know if I've got a right, but I do

have a letter of recommendation. . . . (*The others ad-lib an
argument as she reads her letter.*) "Being possessed of multiple
emotional trauma, it is here by recommended that . . . (*actress's
name*) . . . sings the blues to the fullest extent allowable by the
laws of this state." (*They sing.*)

ALL.
OH — I'VE MADE A WRECK OF
MY LIFE IN EVERY WAY,
SO — I'M PAGING CHEKOV.
I'M A BLUES-ED UP MAMA —
USE ME IN A DRAMA.
    SECOND ACTRESS.
DON'T EVER TRY TO HEAL ME.
    FIRST and SECOND ACTRESSES.
DON'T NORMAN VINCENT PEALE ME.
    ALL.
JUST LEAVE ME IN MY JUICES TO STEW,
    THIRD ACTRESS.
I'M GONNA BE AS MAUDLIN
AS THE LAW WILL ALLOW.
    FIRST and SECOND ACTRESSES.
AND HOW!
    ALL.
'CAUSE I GOT A CONFESSION,
THIS IS A GREAT DEPRESSION.
I'M BLUER THAN THOU!
YA SHOULDN'T EVEN KNOW FROM
WHAT I'VE BEEN THROUGH. . . .

I'M BLUE — AIN'T THESE TEARS TELLIN' YOU?
I'M BLUE — I'M BLUER THAN YOU.
I'M BLUE — I'M BLUE.

I'M BLUER THAN
BLUER THAN
BLUER THAN
BLUER THAN YOU. . . . Don't ask!
(*They exit, griping and complaining.*)

END OF ACT I

ACT TWO

WATCHING THE PRETTY YOUNG MEN

Lights come up to reveal three chairs set in a semicircle. Cocktail lounge music plays under as ARLENE, ROZ, and HELEN enter, clutching purses.

ARLENE. Are you sure the parking lot is open all night? The last train is at 10:40 and if we miss it we'll be stuck here all night. .

ROZ. (*cutting her off*) Arlene, will you stop already? The parking lot is open all night. Now *this* is a great table! (*They begin to settle into the chairs.*)

HELEN. I didn't know we'd be so close to the stage.

ROZ. They say there is one guy here who is really . . (*She makes a suggestive gesture.*)

ARLENE. (*trying to exit*) I have to call the sitter. (*The others stop her.*)

ROZ. I don't believe it.

HELEN. Arlene, you're making me nervous. Sit down.

ROZ. Anybody has to go to the ladies' room do it now while I order the drinks. (*The lights dim as an anticipatory chord is heard. The women slump in various attitudes of anticipation and embarrassment.*) Too late.

ARLENE. Oh, my God.

HELEN. Oh, my God.

ROZ. Oh, my God.

ALL. (*singing*)
OKAY, ALL RIGHT,
THIS IS GONNA BE THE NIGHT.
I GUESS WE'RE IN FOR QUITE AN EXPERIENCE —
CURTAIN UP, THERE GOES THE LIGHT.
AND OH, MY GOD! JUST LOOK AT THAT!
A G-STRING AND A COWBOY HAT!

(*The following is done first as individual solos, then repeated as a round.*)

ROZ.
HEY, HEY, HEY, YOU'RE DRIVIN' ME CRAZY
WHEN YOU MOVE SO LAZY, YOU MOVE SO HOT!
ARLENE.
MOTHERS DON'T GO TO THIS KIND OF SHOW.

THEY STAY HOME WITH CHILDREN AND BAKE
  CUPCAKES A LOT.
HELEN.
COME AND SHOW YOUR MAMA HOW SWEET YOU ARE,
AND SHE'LL TAKE YOU RIDING IN HER CADILLAC
  CAR.

(*HELEN takes a pair of binoculars out of her bag. ARLENE
  nudges her and she puts them away.*)

ALL.
THIS CAN'T BE ME,
I CAN GUARANTEE.
IT SEEMS SO WELL, YOU KNOW, UNINHIBITED.
WHO'D HAVE THOUGHT I'D EVER BE.
AND OH, MY GOD JUST LOOK AT THOSE!
I WONDER HOW THEY'D LOOK IN CLOTHES!

(*ROZ stands and starts to walk toward the performers. AR-
  LENE pulls her back. The following is done as a round,
  with each person moving on to the next verse on each pro-
  gression until they arrive back at the original verse.*)

ROZ. (*Verse 1*)
HEY, HEY, HEY, YOU'RE DRIVIN' ME CRAZY
WHEN YOU MOVE SO LAZY, YOU MOVE SO HOT.

(*When HELEN sings this verse, she pulls out a telescope to
  look at the men.*)

ARLENE. (*Verse 2*)
BABY IS BAD, AND MAMA IS GLAD
'CAUSE IT'S OH, SO WICKED WHEN YOU SHAKE IT A
  LOT.

HELEN. (*Verse 3*)
COME AND SHOW YOUR MAMA HOW SWEET YOU
  ARE,
AND SHE'LL TAKE YOU RIDING IN HER CADILLAC
  CAR.
(*HELEN takes out her car keys and waves them at the dancers.*)
ALL. (*They pull themselves together after their display.*)

OKAY I'M SHY.
I THINK I'D DIE
IF SOMEONE SAW THE WAY I'M BEHAVING NOW,
SAW THE LOOK THAT'S IN MY EYE.
AND OH, MY GOD! THERE'S MARY STEIF,
WITH MRS. SCHWAB, THE RABBI'S WIFE.
   Roz. (*pointing to the rabbi's wife*)
HEY, HEY, HEY IT'S DRIVING THEM CRAZY
WHEN THEY MOVE SO LAZY, THEY GET SO HOT.
   Roz and ARLENE.
IF THEY KNEW WE SAW THEM HERE, OOH,
THEY'D BE SHOCKED AND HORRIFIED
AND HEAVEN KNOWS WHAT.
   HELEN.
STILL AND ALL, MY DEARS, THE ODDS ARE EIGHT
   TO TEN,
COME NEXT WEDNESDAY NIGHT, WE'RE GONNA SEE
   THEM AGAIN!

(*The three ladies become very demonstrative, throwing money
   at the dancers, swinging their purses in mid-air, and jump-
   ing onto the chairs.*)

   ALL.
HEY, HEY, HEY, YOU'RE DRIVING ME CRAZY
WHEN YOU MOVE SO LAZY, YOU MOVE SO HOT.
HEY, HEY, HEY, YOU'RE DRIVING ME CRAZY
WHEN YOU MOVE SO LAZY, YOU MOVE SO HOT.

(*The stage lights dim and the house lights come back up. The
   women pull themselves together.*)

WATCHING ALL THE PRETTY YOUNG MEN—
WE ARE WATCHING ALL THE PRETTY YOUNG MEN.
WATCHING ALL THE PRETTY YOUNG MEN,
WATCHING . . .
   ARLENE. (*speaking*) Next Wednesday, girls? (*They nod in
eager agreement, singing—*)
ALL THE PRETTY YOUNG MEN!
(*Blackout*)

DEMIGOD

A WOMAN enters and crosses to c. *stage.*

WOMAN. I know you're gonna go. . . . I know it. I've been thinking a lot about what you said and I believe that you love me too. . . . And I understand that she gives you something else, something you need I guess is what you said. I wanted to apologize for yesterday. I was so confused, you know. I didn't know what to do with myself. . . . I mean, two years . . . what does a person do? Do I have a nervous breakdown? Do I start a new career? Do I go and have an affair with O.J. Simpson? I mean what do I do? I felt so ugly, Frank, and I don't mean just looks, I mean ugly . . . you know? Then you held me and touched the back of my neck and kissed me and said the things you said, and I felt a lot better. So, I did our laundry, like I always do on Sundays. And in the middle of folding our bedspread, I noticed your jock strap in the washing machine. Drowning in the wash cycle. It was twisting and turning, being mangled and manipulated into all sorts of painful positions. It looked as if it were crying out for help, poor little thing. Then the strangest thing . . . I imagined you were still in it . . . the jock strap I mean. I got hysterical. I mean I couldn't stop laughing. I thought it was the funniest thing I ever thought of. . . . People started staring at me. . . . A woman came up to me and said I should be careful not to inhale too much of that fabric softener. . . . Then all of a sudden I heard your voice. So I ran over to the machine, lifted the lid, and I could hear you in there, choking on the Clorox 2 and the Lemon Fab. But I couldn't make out what you were saying, so I yelled, "Frank, what is it, what are you saying?" And the manager of the laundromat yelled back, "I'm gonna call the police if you don't stop screamin' at your wash, lady!" It made me think, Frank. It made me think that maybe I'm not handling this too well. I can't drop two years of being lovers and go back to being friends. We never were friends, Frank. We slept together on the first date, remember? And I know you wanted to leave on good terms, like telling me you still love me and all, but I really think it'll be easier for me if we break up as enemies. It'll be better for me just to hate you openly instead of being so adult about it, don't you think? I mean, why be adult about it? So we can meet for lunch and laugh about all this? So you can tell me about your lovers and I can tell you about my lovers? So we can sleep together for old times' sake? I don't want to be your friend,

Frank. I loved you, but I never said I liked you. And if being adult means throwing *me* away for that slut-rag you picked up on the goddamned train platform, then the most mature thing I could do for you would be to rip your face off. (*She mimes doing so.*) Oh, yes! That feels much better! (*Blackout*)

THE FRENCH MONOLOGUE

An ACTRESS enters DS.R., *wearing a beret and carrying a lighted cigarette in a long elegant holder. She is very, very French. She speaks directly to the audience in a thick French accent.*

ACTRESS Hello you . . . remember me? Chanteuse Rosé? The little girl with the big voice who died for love—twice a night? Oh, how I love to sing of love—*en Français* of course French is the language of love Of course, I was not always French Until I was thirteen, I was German Being German was nice—I liked the sausage—but in my heart, I knew something was missing So, at thirteen I decided to change For a while I was Danish *Comme ci, comme ça*—I liked the pastry Then I was very many things I was Irish, Italian, Rumanian, Polish, but always, no matter how good the food, or how high the mountains, I knew something was missing—*l'amour n'est-ce pas?* I needed to sing of my broken heart, to die for love—twice a night And for this I needed a slit in my skirt, a beret on my head, long cigarette, champagne, stiletto heels—I needed, I *needed* to be French French—my Papa was right When I was a little girl, he used to come into my room, kneel by my bed, and whisper into my ear, he would say, "Heidi—I was still German then—Heidi, you're different, you should be French " And then he would sing me a little lullaby that never failed to help me to sleep, and so my friends, tonight I would like to sing for you my Papa's lullaby to me that he sang, *en Français* Monsieur? (*Piano player begins as she turns* US *and a single spot picks her up*)

THE FRENCH SONG

ACTRESS.
PARLEZ-VOUS FRANÇAIS, CHANSON PARIS—
FILET MIGNON, N'EST-CE PAS?
MON AMI, CHAISE LOUNGE, CAFÉ À CRÈME,

ESCARGOT, YUM-YUM, POURQUOI?
BEAUJOLAIS, DÉCOR, CHEVROLET COUPÉ —
MERCI, MADAME POMPIDOU,
JEAN COCTEAU TOUT DE SUITE.
(*The lights gradually fill the stage.*)

MON DIEU POTPOURRI —
AH, DAT'S A NICE-A RAGOUT.
À LA MODE, À LA CARTE,
VIVE LA FRANCE.
BON APPETIT, LA GUERRE
CRÊPES SUZETTE, LAFAYETTE
PARDONNEZ-MOI.
C'EST LA VIE, VIN ORDINAIRE.
QU'EST-CE QUE C'EST, COUP DE GRACE —
GO MOW ZE LAWN.
MAURICE CHEVALIER, QUEL BOEUF,
VERSAILLES EN CHANTÉ, LA PLUME DE MA TANTE,
CHATEAUBRIAND, C'EST TOUGH.

LIBERTÉ, EGALITÉ, FRATERNITÉ —
FAUT PAS AU COCO CHANEL.
VOULEZ-VOUS COUCHER
AVEC MOI CE SOIR?
NO BIDET EN LE HOTEL.
(*The lights narrow to just the* c. *stage spot.*)

COQ AU VIN, IMMEDIATEMENT —
ARC DE TRIOMPHE
MON PLAISIR, CHAMPS D'ÉLYSÉES
COURTERIER C'EST NOM
MERDE IN LE CHAPEAU.
J'ACCUSE, JACQUELINE BOUVIER!
(*spoken*) Good-night Papa! (*She exits* US.C. *as lights blackout.*)

PAY THEM NO MIND

An ACTRESS enters US.C. *The song starts low-key and gradually builds until it is triumphant at the end.*

ACTRESS.
PEOPLE LAUGH EACH TIME THEY SEE US PASSING BY

AND THEIR WHISPERING MAKES YOU FEEL LIKE YOU
    WANT TO CRY.
KEEP ON WALKING BY MY SIDE, DON'T LOOK
    BEHIND —
YOU SEE, I LOVE YOU, SO PAY THEM NO MIND.

PEOPLE SAY OUR LOVE AIN'T GONNA LAST TOO
    LONG,
AND THEY POINT AT US AS THOUGH WE'VE BEEN
    ONLY CARRYING ON.
KEEP ON LOOKING IN MY EYES, AND WE'LL BE FINE.
'CAUSE I LOVE YOU, SO PAY THEM NO MIND.

STAY WITH ME AND LET THEM SEE,
LET THEM KNOW THAT YOU LOVE ME.
IF IT'S TRUE, WHO CARES WHAT THEY DO,
'CAUSE I DON'T NEED ANYONE BUT YOU.

IT'S YOU AND ME, WE'RE GONNA MAKE IT ALL
    ALONE
SO LET THEM LAUGH AT US, WE'RE GONNA BUILD
    A WORLD ALL OUR OWN.
HOLD ON, HOLD ON TO ME, THEY'LL LEARN IN TIME.
HOW I LOVE YOU, SO PAY THEM NO MIND.

STAY WITH ME AND LET THEM SEE,
LET THEM KNOW THAT YOU LOVE ME.
IF IT'S TRUE, WHO CARES WHAT THEY DO,
'CAUSE I DON'T NEED ANYONE BUT YOU.

IT'S YOU AND ME, WE'RE GONNA MAKE IT ALL
    ALONE.
SO LET THEM LAUGH AT US, WE'RE GONNA BUILD
    A WORLD ALL OUR OWN.
HOLD ON, HOLD ON TO ME, THEY'LL LEARN IN TIME.
HOW I LOVE YOU, SO PAY THEM NO MIND.

STAY WITH ME AND LET THEM SEE,
LET THEM KNOW THAT YOU LOVE ME.
IF IT'S TRUE, WHO CARES WHAT THEY DO,
'CAUSE I DON'T NEED ANYONE BUT YOU.

IT'S YOU AND ME, WE'RE GONNA BUILD A WORLD ALL
OUR OWN.
HOLD ON, HOLD ON TO ME, THEY'LL LEARN IN TIME.
KEEP ON WALKING BY MY SIDE, DON'T STOP, DON'T
LOOK BEHIND YOU.
HOLD ON, HOLD ON TO ME, THEY'LL LEARN IN TIME.
HOW I LOVE YOU, SO PAY THEM NO MIND.
(*Blackout*)

HOT LUNCH

The WORKMAN enters DS.L. *and sits on a bit of construction
debris. He wears a hard hat and carries a metal lunch box
that he eats from. He ogles the imaginary girls that walk by.*

WORKMAN. Wowee, would I like a taste of that . . . beautiful,
baby, beautiful . . . Hey, don't ignore me, honey; you're not
that pretty. . . . (*A WOMAN enters and crosses past him.*)
Wowie, look at them gazoombas! I'd like to show you a taste of
heaven, honey bunny.

WOMAN. (*very polite*) Excuse me, would you repeat what you
just said to me?

WORKMAN. (*startled*) Huh? Oh sure. I said I'd like to show
you a taste of heaven, honey bunny.

WOMAN. What else? You said something before that I couldn't
quite make out.

WORKMAN. (*getting annoyed*) I don't know. I said you got a
great pair of legs or something. I forget.

WOMAN. (*matter of fact*) No, no, I don't think you said legs
. . . . It was something more like daroombas.

WORKMAN. Hey lady, walk on by will ya? I'm eating my
lunch.

WOMAN. Yes, and I'm very sorry to disturb you, but try to
remember what you said. It's very important to me. . . . Now, it
sounded like . . .

WORKMAN. (*very softly*) Gazoombas.

WOMAN. Sorry, I didn't get that.

WORKMAN. Gazoombas! Now will you please leave me alone?
I'm on my lunch break.

WOMAN. I know, I know I'm infringing on your time and I
apologize for it, but what are gazoombas?

WORKMAN. Aw, just a word. A made-up word. No big deal.

Look if you're pissed off I'm sorry, okay? I said gazoombas, so what? You got a nice shape. Since when is it a crime to give a compliment?

WOMAN. Yes, yes, I understand your motivation. It's just the word, gazoombas. I'd never heard it before. What exactly does gazoombas refer to?

WORKMAN. (*embarrassed*) You know. (*indicates up*) Up there. (*She looks up.*) Your chest, lady.

WOMAN. (*relieved*) Oh, thank goodness. I kind of thought that's what you meant, but I wasn't quite sure.

WORKMAN. Well, that's what I meant, okay? No offense. (*He begins to pack up.*)

WOMAN. Of course not. (*She sits very close to him abruptly.*) So, you like my tits.

WORKMAN. (*Startled, he jumps up.*) Hey, cool it, will you? I work here!

WOMAN. Sorry, I just wanted to know if you really appreciated my mammaries.

WORKMAN. Lady, would you excuse me? I gotta get back on the job. (*He tries to go past her and she stops him with her hands on his shoulders.*)

WOMAN. Of course, how stupid of me. But before you go, I'd like you to see my gazoombas! (*With back to audience, she opens her blouse to him.*)

WORKMAN. Lady, lady, cover yourself! What are you doing!

WOMAN. I thought if I showed you my gazoombas, you'd show me your wogabongo. (*He covers his crotch with the lunch box.*)

WORKMAN. Wogabongo?

WOMAN. You know . . . your pecker, dick, schlong, johnson . . . wogabooongo!!!

WORKMAN. (*trying to leave*) You're a wacko lady!

WOMAN. Why am I a wacko? You like my gazoombas, I like your wagabongo. I just want that taste of heaven you promised me. Why, with my gazoombas and your wogabongo, we could make great shtahpoonko!

WORKMAN. (*calling to his unseen coworker*) Hey, Joe! Joe! Help! Help!

WOMAN. (*really going for him*) C'mon, Wogabongo, squeeze my gazoombas!

WORKMAN. (*running for the exit*) Help, Joe, call the cops! I got a nut-case down here! Help!

WOMAN. (*chasing after him*) Oh, baby boy, I can't wait to show you my chubookie!

WORKMAN. Oh, my God!!!! (*He exits. The WOMAN, thoroughly pleased with herself, straightens herself up, dusts off her hands, and exits in the other direction, happy with a job well done.*)

(*Blackout*)

FOR WOMEN ONLY #3

The POETESS enters US.C. *and crosses* DS. *once again lugging the book.*

POETESS. The final poem from my collection. Autographed copies will be available in the lobby following the performance.
I am woman.
A dying swan.
Dancing, dancing, dancing.
My toe shoes torn.
My tutu, too.
He did it.
He did it.
(And he knows who he is.)
That weekend he took her skiing
in Aspen—
That's when he did it.

A love bullet through my feathered breast.
(*thumps book*)

I am woman.
A dying swan.

Ach-ch
(*Lights start to fade.*)

Ach-ch
Ach-ch
Ach—
(*Lights are out.*)

EMILY THE M.B.A.

This is performed in the style of a tough Sixties girl-group.
The four WOMEN in this group are just as tough—they
wear suit jackets and carry briefcases.

CHORUS. (*singing*)
DOO-DOO-DOO-DOO-DOO.
CHORUS LEADER. (*speaking*) Emily majored in finance. She
trained for the fastest track. First in her class, summa cum
laude, she was:
EMILY. (*singing*)
THE ACHIEVER OF THE PACK.
CHORUS LEADER. (*speaking*) Emily's class was distinguished.
For the first time the school was co-ed. The valedictorian was
Emmy. . . .
ALL. (*singing*)
AND AT GRADUATION SHE SAID:
EMILY. (*addressing her class*)
NOW WE GO FORTH INTO BUSINESS,
NOW WE ARE MS. M.B.A.
WE MUSTN'T LOSE SIGHT OF OUR MS-NESS.
LET'S ALL TAKE A VOW TODAY:

(*Each CHORUS MEMBER, as she starts to sing along with
EMILY, takes a vow.*)

REMEMBER WE'VE GOT TO BE DIFFERENT,
REMEMBER WE'VE GOT TO BE NEW,
REMEMBER WE'VE GOT TO CHANGE ALL OF IT,
BUT BE SURE WHAT GETS CHANGED,
ISN'T YOU.
CHORUS LEADER.
EMILY SOON WAS RECRUITED
BY TRON-MEGA-TECH-DATA-BASE.
BOW-TIED AND CORPORATELY SUITED,
SHE INSCRIBED ON HER ATTACHÉ CASE:
EMILY.
REMEMBER WE'VE GOT TO BE DIFFERENT.
CHORUS.
DOO-DOO-DOO-DOO.

EMILY and CHORUS LEADER.
REMEMBER WE'VE GOT TO BE NEW.
ALL.
REMEMBER WE'VE GOT TO CHANGE ALL OF IT,
BUT BE SURE WHAT GETS CHANGED
ISN'T YOU.

(*The CHORUS dances with their briefcases as they sing "Go, go, Emily!"*)

FIRST CHORUS MEMBER. (*speaking in 60's street-fighting bad-girl style*) Did Emily progress vertically through the corporate structure?
CHORUS LEADER. Best believe it, girl. Within a year she was handling acquisitions.
SECOND CHORUS MEMBER. (*challenging*) Oh, yeah? How did Emily deal with take-overs?
EMILY. I was good-bad, but I wasn't evil.
FIRST CHORUS MEMBER. Yeah, well how did Emily play corporate politics?
CHORUS LEADER. Close . . . very, very close. (*They hurl their briefcases offstage. Then they continue the song.*)
CHORUS LEADER.
BUT EMMY'S PROGRESS STARTED SLOWING.
HER CAREER BEGAN PLATEAU-ING.
(*EMILY begins to get worried.*)
EMILY.
OH, NO!
CHORUS.
OH, NO! OH, NO!
CHORUS LEADER.
SHE THOUGHT A LITTLE SELF-ENHANCEMENT
MIGHT REVITALIZE ADVANCEMENT.
EMILY.
OH, YEAH!
CHORUS.
OH, YEAH. OH, YEAH.
CHORUS LEADER.
SOMETHING REALLY SPLASHY,
THAT'S WHAT SHE WOULD DO.
EMILY.
ENGINEER A FLASHY
ACQUISITION COUP.

ALL. (*getting excited by the idea*)
OOOH-OOOH-OOOH-OOOH . . .
CHORUS LEADER.
WHERE WAS THE PROSPECT EMMY WONDERED
THAT WAS RIPE FOR GETTING PLUNDERED?
EMILY.
UNDER.
CHORUS.
UNDER, UNDER.
CHORUS LEADER.
WHERE WAS THE OUTFIT SO FORSAKEN
IT WAS ACHIN' TO BE TAKEN?
EMILY.
OVER.
CHORUS.
OVER, OVER.
CHORUS LEADER.
SHE FOUND THE FIRM TO STOMP ON,
(*EMILY smiles.*)
THE COMPANY TO SINK,
THE ONE THAT SHE WOULD TROMP ON WAS . . .
EMILY.
WOMAN TRONICS INC!

(*The CHORUS is horrified at EMILY doing in a company run by women.*)

CHORUS.
OH, NO, NO, NO, NO, NO, EMILY!
(*They back away from EMILY.*)
REMEMBER, DOO-DOO-DOO. . . .
EMILY. (*speaking, to CHORUS*) What do you mean, "No, no, Emily." I'm not going to pass this up just because it's a company run by women. You're asking me to put my career on the line. A male executive wouldn't have to think twice about this. (*delivering the big one*) Business is business!
CHORUS LEADER. (*singing*)
THE TAKE-OVER STRUGGLE WAS STRESSFUL!
CHORUS.
STRESSFUL!
CHORUS LEADER.
BUT TO EMILY WINNING WAS ALL!

CHORUS.
WINNING, WINNING WAS ALL!
CHORUS LEADER.
SHE SAID WHEN HER PLAN WAS SUCCESSFUL—
CHORUS.
WHAT SHE SAY?
EMILY.
LET'S GO THERE AND WATCH THEM CRAWL!

(*During the following dialogue, the CHORUS acts out the action as the CHORUS LEADER narrates it. The CHORUS sings "No, no, Emily" under.*)

CHORUS LEADER. Emily and two guys from upper management took off in a company car to close the take-over deal. On the way, they broke out a bottle of Chivas, and a toast was proposed: To Emily!
CHORUS. (*toasting*) Emily!
CHORUS LEADER. One toast followed another as dark clouds filled the sky! Was it the rain or was it the Regal? No one saw the sign that said: Danger! Bridge Collapse!
ALL. Watch out watch out watch out watch out!

(*Pandemonium breaks out. The CHORUS whirls and shrieks. Lights flash on and off. Car crash sound effect. EMILY spins offstage. When all is quiet, a lone hub cap clatters across the stage. The group reforms and begins a slow funeral march. The CHORUS sobs gently as the CHORUS LEADER sings.*)

CHORUS LEADER.
THAT EVENING THEY PULLED FROM THE WRECKAGE
THREE TWISTED BODIES, ALL DEAD.
AND THEY FOUND IN THAT CORPORATE EXECAGE—
CHORUS. (*speaking*) What they find?
CHORUS LEADER.
AN INSCRIBED PIECE OF LEATHER THAT READ:
ALL. (*once again taking the vow*)
REMEMBER WE'VE GOT TO BE DIFFERENT.
REMEMBER WE'VE GOT TO BE NEW.
REMEMBER WE'VE GOT TO CHANGE ALL OF IT.
BUT BE SURE WHAT GETS CHANGED

OH, NO, NO,
ISN'T
OH NO NO NO NO NO NO NO NO,
ISN'T YOU!
(*Blackout*)

SISTERS

An ACTRESS enters and sits c. stage. She sings.

MY SISTER AND I, WE SHARE AN APARTMENT IN
   QUEENS.
WE MOVED FROM THE VILLAGE WHEN IT WENT WAY
   BEYOND OUR MEANS.
HER HUSBAND DIVORCED HER AND LEFT TOWN IN
   SEVENTY-ONE.
HE SAID THAT HE NEEDED A YOUNGER GIRL WHO
   WAS MORE FUN.

I LOST MY JOEY, LET'S SEE, YES, IT'S EIGHT YEARS
   TODAY.
THE HURT WAS SO BAD THAT I'VE LOCKED ALL MY
   MEM'RIES AWAY.
WE TRY NOT TO FOCUS OUR EYES OR OUR HEARTS ON
   THE PAST,
OR MENTION NOSTALGICALLY HOW TIME GOES
   FLYING SO FAST.

SHE WAS THE PRETTY ONE, I WAS THE ONE WHO
   COULD SING.
I SOUGHT THE FAME AND THE LOVE I THOUGHT
   BEAUTY COULD BRING.
SHE SEEMED SO SURE OF HERSELF, WHILE I FELT SO
   AFRAID,
SHE THOUGHT IF SHE HAD MY TALENT SHE'D SURE
   HAVE IT MADE.

NEVER CONNECTING, WE LIVED OUR ADULTHOODS
   ALONE,
SHE WAS SELF-SATISFIED, I PROUD TO BE ON MY
   OWN.

FUNNY HOW LIFE BRINGS THE BEST OF US DOWN
  TO OUR KNEES.
FUNNY HOW HEARTS CAN PERCEIVE WHAT THE EYE
  NEVER SEES.

SOMEHOW WE TOUCHED IN THE DARKNESS OF
  LONELY AND OLD.
JEALOUSY FADES WHEN TWO STORIES ARE ALREADY
  TOLD.
JOY TIPTOES IN SOMETIMES AS LIFE'S SURPRISES
  ARRIVE.
MY SISTER AND I – WE ARE SHARING THE END OF
  OUR LIVES.
(*The lights slowly dim.*)

HONEYPOT

*A single spot comes up to reveal a blues singer decked out à
  la Billie Holiday, with a flower in her hair. She sings in various blues styles.*

HONEYPOT.
OH, WON'T YOU HELP ME,
WON'T YOU HELP ME PLEASE?
I GOT AN ACHIN'
THAT'S SHAKIN'
ME DOWN TO MY KNEES.

OH, WON'T YOU TELL ME
WHAT THIS MIGHT BE?
IS IT THE SAME OLD THING THAT'S
ALWAYS WRONG WITH ME?

(*Lights come up to reveal the interior of a psychotherapist's
  office. The doctor is very "modern" and serious, and takes
  notes occasionally.*)

DOCTOR. (*speaking*) Well, I'm here to help. So please, feel
free to say exactly what's on your mind. (*HONEYPOT sits by
the DOCTOR's desk.*)
HONEYPOT. (*singing*)
I WANT SOME SWEETMEAT, DADDY.

COME AND DIP IT IN MY BOWL.
I NEED THAT JELLY ROLL, DADDY.
COME ON AND FILL MY DONUT HOLE.

MY COFFEE'S BEEN SITTIN'
FOR WEEKS ON THE SHELF.
IF YOU DON'T COME BY AND GRIND IT
I MUST DO IN MYSELF.

I NEED THAT SWEETMEAT, DADDY. . . .

DOCTOR. (*speaking*) I'm not sure I understand exactly, Miss . . .

HONEYPOT. Honeypot.

DOCTOR. Yes, well, Miss Pott, I was wondering if . . .

HONEYPOT. No, Honeypot's my first name. Honeypot Watkins, the blues singer. (*riff on the piano*)

DOCTOR. Well, Honeypot, you seem to have some sense of your personal desires, but I wonder if you could tell me *exactly* what it is you want.

HONEYPOT. (*singing*)
I WANT SOME SWEETMEAT, DADDY,
COME ON AND DIP IT . . .

DOCTOR. (*speaking*) Honeypot, I'm going to be frank. You're trying to articulate your sexual needs, aren't you?

HONEYPOT. (*a bit embarrassed*) Well, yes, Doctor, I guess I am. . . .

DOCTOR. Fine. But what I'm hearing is a lot of talk about food. Do you think you could discuss sex without referring to the contents of your refrigerator?

HONEYPOT. I think so.

DOCTOR. Well, then, why don't I ask you again? What is it exactly you want?

HONEYPOT. (*singing*)
WHEN MY OVEN'S OVERHEATED
I NEED MY FIXIT MAN.
WHEN MY LOCK NEEDS OPENIN',
I'M SURE HE'S THE ONE WHO CAN.

HE'S GOT A MONKEY WRENCH
THAT I LOVE TO USE.
DON'T KNOW HOW I'D LIVE
WITHOUT HIS SCREWS.

OH, HE'S MY HANDY, DANDY
FIXIT MAN,
YEAH, YEAH, YEAH . . .

DOCTOR. (*interrupts, speaking*) Let me ask you . . . do you often find yourself associating sex with food and hardware?

HONEYPOT. No, I really haven't noticed that.

DOCTOR. Then do you think we could try once again? You know, Honeypot, we're all a little embarrassed to really discuss sexuality. That's a perfectly normal response. (*HONEYPOT is relieved.*) But if you'd like to try to work through that . . .

HONEYPOT. Oh, yes, I'd love to try to work through that.

DOCTOR. Please, feel free. What sorts of sexual activities do you most enjoy?

HONEYPOT. (*singing*)
HE COMES TO MY STABLE,
GRAZES IN MY HAY.
HE REARS UP, NICE AND HIGH
AND OHHH. . . .
I LIKE IT THAT WAY, YEAH, YEAH!
I LIKE IT THAT WAY, YEAH, YEAH. . . .

DOCTOR. (*speaking*) Try not to mention horses.

HONEYPOT. (*groping for another approach, speaking*) Okay . . . (*singing*)
DIVE DOWN, DADDY
YOU NEVER MISS A STROKE.
WHY DON'T YOU
DIVE DOWN, DADDY . . .

DOCTOR. Try not to mention swimming.

HONEYPOT. (*speaking*) Okay. Uhhh . . . (*singing*)
I GOT A REAL THING FOR THAT THING.
IT REALLY MAKES MY SPIRIT SING.
I GOT A REAL THING FOR THAT THING. . . .

DOCTOR. (*getting excited*) All right, what *thing* is that exactly, Honeypot?

HONEYPOT. Well, you know what I mean, his . . . oh, you know.

DOCTOR. His penis. Right? (*HONEYPOT is horrified.*)

HONEYPOT. Ahh! Yes, his monkey wrench!

DOCTOR. Yes, his monkey wrench. But you mean something else when you say that.

HONEYPOT. (*forcing out the word*) His . . . p . . . penis?

DOCTOR. Yes. Now, what would you like him to do with the penis?

HONEYPOT. (*singing*)
DADDY, MY DOOR'S WIDE OPEN.
WHY DON'T YOU COME ON INSIDE?
DADDY, MY DOOR SWINGS EASY. . . .

DOCTOR. (*flatly*) You can think before you answer, you know.

HONEYPOT. (*trying to please*) Doctor, I think I know what you mean.

DOCTOR. (*excited*) Yes?

HONEYPOT. I think I want the *penis* . . .

DOCTOR. Yes?

HONEYPOT. (*speaking*) In my . . . (*singing*)
SUGARBOWL. . . .

DOCTOR. (*an accusatory silence*)

HONEYPOT. (*softly*) Vagina.

DOCTOR. This is very important, Honeypot! Are you feeling yourself becoming more aware of what it is you really want? That it isn't wrenches and donuts?

HONEYPOT. Yes, I think so.

DOCTOR. Can you tell me about it?

HONEYPOT. (*speaking*) Yes, I believe I can. (*singing operatically, and standing in a classical singing pose*)
I'D LIKE EXTENDED FOREPLAY, DADDY,
NOT MERELY GENITAL CONTACT AS SUCH.
THEN PROCEED WITH ACTUAL PENETRATION,
    DADDY.
I'D ENJOY THAT VERY MUCH.

I'D LIKE TO EXPERIENCE SEXUAL RELEASE
CONCURRENTLY WITH YOU.
I'D PREFER A MULTIPLE CLIMAX
BUT THE OTHER KIND WILL DO.

CONSIDER SEX JUST ONE ASPECT OF ME AS A
    PERSON, DADDY. . . .

DOCTOR. (*speaking*) Wonderful progress, Honeypot.

HONEYPOT. Thank you, Doctor.

DOCTOR. With regular therapy, within five years you should have a sex life as good as the typical American woman.

HONEYPOT. (*A look of horror passes over HONEYPOT's face. She slips back into her blues style of singing.*)
COME BACK HERE, DADDY,
AND PUT THAT MONEKY WRENCH IN MY BOWL!
(*She exits. Lights fade.*)

FRIENDS

Two ACTRESSES are discovered sitting a little apart. Throughout the piece, as they gradually age, they occasionally change position in their chairs. They do not look at each other until the very end.

OFFSTAGE VOICE. Are you still on that phone?

FIRST ACTRESS. (*speaking*)	SECOND ACTRESS. (*speaking*)
	You hang up first.
Okay . . . you still there?	
	No fair. I did last time.
Well. . . . (*singing*) DON'T FORGET, CALL ME IN THE MORNING.	(*singing*)
	BE MY FRIEND.
TELL ME WHAT YOU'RE GONNA WEAR TO SCHOOL	
	THOSE STUCK UP GIRLS.
HELP ME WITH MY MATH. I'LL DO YOUR ENGLISH.	
	THE BOYS
PLEASE DON'T TELL YOUR BROTHER I THINK HE'S COOL. DON'T FORGET, CALL ME IN THE MORNING. (*speaking*)	DON'T FORGET, CALL ME IN THE MORNING. (*speaking*) Maid of Honor?
Of course! Matron of Honor?	

Oh, wow.
Lamaze?

I'll try.
Aerobics?

(*singing*)

I'll try.
(*singing*)
DON'T FORGET.
I NEED YOUR PLUMBER'S
    NUMBER.

THE CHILDREN.

MEET YOU AT THE
    PLAYGROUND
AROUND ONE.

OH, GOD, THE HOUSE.

HOW DO YOU FIND TIME
TO READ A NOVEL?

MY HUSBAND.

THOUGHT I'D WORK
    FREELANCE
BUT WOMAN'S WORK IS
    NEVER DONE.
WELL,

DON'T FORGET,   DON'T FORGET,
CALL ME IN THE   CALL ME IN THE
    MORNING   MORNING

YOU REMEMBER MY
    FIRST LOVE
MY DRESS SIZE
MY BIRTHDAY
MY DIVORCE

OF COURSE I DO
AND YOU KNOW I CAN'T
    EAT GARLIC
AND MY SON-IN-LAW
    BORES ME.

AND SOMETIMES MAYBE
    I DO TOO.

OF COURSE YOU DO.

WELL SOMETIMES
I GET SORE AT YOU.
BUT WHAT THE HELL,

WHAT THE HELL,
WHAT ARE FRIENDS
  FOR?

WHAT ARE FRIENDS
  FOR?

WHAT ARE FRIENDS
  FOR?

WHAT ARE FRIENDS
  FOR?

BE MY FRIEND.
(*speaking*)

BE MY FRIEND.
(*speaking*)
The kids are moving to
  Denver.

Let's go back to school.
(*singing*)
I NEED A FRIEND
(*speaking*)
I can't believe he's gone.

(*singing*)
I NEED A FRIEND.
(*speaking*)

You did everything you
  could.
(*singing*)

(*singing*)
I'LL BE YOUR FRIEND.
I'LL BE YOUR FRIEND.
MY FRIEND, MY FRIEND.

I'LL BE YOUR FRIEND.
I'LL BE YOUR FRIEND.
MY FRIEND, MY FRIEND.

DON'T FORGET, I'LL
COME AND SEE YOU
  SUNDAY

HELLO, FRIEND.

THINK OF SOMEPLACE
  NICE
YOU'D LIKE TO GO.

YOUR GINSENG TEA
IS QUITE A PICK-UP.

A CUP OF TEA.

I MAKE A CUP
WHENEVER I FEEL
  SLOW.

CUP OF TEA.

TASTES FUNNY
  THOUGH.
YOU LISTEN TO THOSE
  NURSES, NOW
YOU KNOW.

MEMORY
IS FUNNY THOUGH.

MY FRIEND,
I KNOW.

AND DON'T FORGET,
   CALL ME IN THE
   MORNING.   FIRST THING IN THE
                             MORNING.

(The two WOMEN look at each other for the first time.)

DON'T FORGET,   DON'T FORGET,
CALL ME IN THE   CALL ME IN THE
   MORNING   MORNING.
             (Lights fade out.)

A special light comes up. The THIRD ACTRESS walks into it.

THIRD ACTRESS. *(speaking)*
A . . . My name is Alice . . .
And I'm all right!
Amen!

(Lights come up on the full stage as the music starts.)

ALL GIRL BAND (Reprise)

FOURTH ACTRESS. *(enters US.C. singing)*
IF YOUR LIFE IS A MESS,
   THIRD ACTRESS.
IF YOU'RE BORED WITH SUCCESS,
   FIRST ACTRESS. *(enters US.C.)*
IF YOUR SHRINK TRIES TO PUT YOU AWAY . . .
   SECOND ACTRESS. *(enters DS.R.)*
IF THEY THROW YOU IN JAIL,
   ALL.
OR YOU'VE BROKEN A NAIL,
   FIFTH ACTRESS. *(enters DS.L.)*
OR YOU'VE DENTED YOUR NEW CHEVROLET! . . .
   ALL.
WE HAVE GOT SOME SOUND ADVICE TO PULL YOU
   THROUGH.
THERE'S A VIRTUSO LOCKED INSIDE OF YOU!

COME JOIN OUR ALL-GIRL BAND.
IT'S THE FEMINIST WAY TO RELAX.

COME JOIN OUR ALL-GIRL BAND,
WE NEED A TUBA AND SAX!

COME JOIN OUR ALL-GIRL BAND,
AND THE HARMONY SOARS THROUGH THE NIGHT.
COME JOIN OUR ALL-GIRL BAND.
   FIRST and SECOND ACTRESSES.
NOW I CAN BLOW MY OWN HORN!
   THIRD ACTRESS.
NOW I AM SINGING THE LEAD!
   FOURTH and FIFTH ACTRESSES.
NOW LOOK WHO'S PULLING THE STRINGS!
   ALL.
ALICE IS DOING ALL RIGHT!

(*Jam session*)

   ALL.
ALICE IS DOING ALL RIGHT!
(*Blackout*)

CHARACTER BREAKDOWN

First Actress — Mature, thirtyish black woman. Earthy, but with a strong ironic edge.

Second Actress — Twentyish urban type. Sexy and sometimes neurotic.

Third Actress — Twentyish black woman. Dancer with high energy and sparkling personality.

Fourth Actress — Fiftyish. Warm, motherly type with a mischievous sense of humor.

Fifth Actress — Late twenties/early thirties. Cosmopolitan, sophisticated woman with a secretly zany side.

CAST ASSIGNMENTS (Original Production)

Opening:
All Girl Band:
First Actress—Alaina Reed
Second Actress—Randy Graff
Third Actress—Charlaine Woodard
Fourth Actress—Roo Brown
Fifth Actress—Mary Gordon Murray

At My Age:
Vicky—Roo Brown
Karen—Randy Graff

Trash:
Mindy—Randy Graff
Mrs. Kaplan—Roo Brown
Howard—Mary Gordon Murray
Stanley—Charlaine Woodard
Offstage Voice—Alaina Reed

For Women Only Poems:
Roo Brown

Good Thing I Learned to Dance:
Charlaine Woodard

Welcome to Kindergarten, Mrs. Johnson:
Mrs. Johnson—Mary Gordon Murray
Ms. Thomas—Roo Brown

I Sure Like the Boys:
Randy Graff

Ms. Mae:
Alaina Reed

Good Sports: Detroit Persons/Educated Feet:
Rosie—Roo Brown
Wanda—Randy Graff
Sheridan—Charlaine Woodard
Vonelle—Alaina Reed
Spike—Mary Gordon Murray

The Portrait:
Mary Gordon Murray

Bluer than You:
First Actress—Alaina Reed
Second Actress—Charlaine Woodard
Third Actress—Randy Graff

Pretty Young Men:
Arlene—Mary Gordon Murray
Roz—Roo Brown
Helen—Alaina Reed

Demigod:
Charlaine Woodard

The French Song and Monologue:
Mary Gordon Murray

Pay Them No Mind:
Alaina Reed

Hot Lunch:
Workman—Mary Gordon Murray
Woman—Charlaine Woodard

Emily the M.B.A.:
Emily—Randy Graff
Chorus Leader—Alaina Reed
First Chorus Member—Mary Gordon Murray
Second Chorus Member—Charlaine Woodard

Sisters:
Roo Brown

Honeypot:
Doctor—Randy Graff
Honeypot—Alaina Reed

Friends:
First Actress—Mary Gordon Murray
Second Actress—Randy Graff

Finale:
All Girl Band:
Same as opening

COSTUME PLOT

Actress #1:

ALL GIRL BAND—Basic Costume: Sophisticated silky dress, shoes to match

TRASH—Off stage

GOOD THING I LEARNED TO DANCE—Off stage

MS. MAE—Over basic costume: Hairdresser's cape, towel over shoulders, "little old lady" shoes & stockings

DETROIT PERSONS/EDUCATED FEET—Over basic costume: fighter's dressing robe, sneakers, socks

BLUER THAN YOU—Basic costume

PRETTY YOUNG MEN—Basic costume

PAY THEM NO MIND—Basic costume, add casual jacket

EMILY THE MBA—Basic costume, add business suit jacket

HONEYPOT—Basic costume, add filmy, lightweight stole

ALL GIRL BAND REPRISE—Basic costume

Actress #2:

ALL GIRL BAND—Basic costume: Casual pants, short-sleeved shirt, casual pull over sweater, flat shoes and socks

AT MY AGE—Basic costume, add denim jacket

TRASH—Basic costume, loose denim jacket, add earrings

I SURE LIKE THE BOYS—Basic pants; soft, slightly sophisticated blouse

DETROIT PERSONS/EDUCATED FEET—Basic shirt, pullover vest, athletic shorts, sneakers and socks

BLUER THAN YOU—Basic costume

EMILY THE MBA—Basic pants, shirt, shoes; add: business suit jacket

HONEYPOT—Basic costume

FRIENDS—Basic costume

ALL GIRL BAND REPRISE—Basic costume

Actress #3:

ALL GIRL BAND—Basic costume: Short, youthful casual skirt, lightweight sweater, shoes to match, leotard under

TRASH—Basic costume, add man's hat & tie, socks, sneakers

GOOD THING I LEARNED TO DANCE—Basic costume w/socks, sneakers and long scarf

DETROIT PERSONS/EDUCATED FEET—Basic costume, add sweatshirt jacket, leg guards, socks and sneakers

BLUER THAN YOU—Basic costume

DEMIGOD—Basic costume; add casual jacket

HOT LUNCH — Same as "Demigod"
EMILY THE MBA — Basic costume, add business suit jacket
ALL GIRL BAND REPRISE — Basic costume

Actress #4:
ALL GIRL BAND — Basic costume: Casual, belted dress, shoes
   to match
AT MY AGE — Basic costume
TRASH — Basic costume, add turban and jacket
FOR WOMEN ONLY POEMS 1-2-3 — Basic costume, add
   fringed shawl
WELCOME TO KINDERGARTEN, MRS. JOHNSON — Basic
   costume, add smock and glasses
EDUCATED FEET/DETROIT PERSONS — Basic costume
PRETTY YOUNG MEN — Basic costume
SISTERS — Basic costume
ALL GIRL BAND REPRISE — Basic costume

Actress #5:
ALL GIRL BAND — Basic costume: Casual, somewhat
   sophisticated jumpsuit; shoes to match
TRASH — Basic costume, add man's suit vest, bowtie, glasses
   & sneakers
WELCOME TO KINDERGARTEN, MRS. JOHNSON — Basic
   costume, add jacket
DETROIT PERSONS/EDUCATED FEET — Basic costume,
   add athletic jacket, leather spikes, sneakers & shoes
THE PORTRAIT — Basic costume
PRETTY YOUNG MEN — Basic costume
THE FRENCH MONOLOGUE & SONG — Basic costume,
   add beret, net gloves, and sequin belt
HOT LUNCH — Workman's jumpsuit, hard hat and sneakers
EMILY THE MBA — Basic costume, add business suit jacket
FRIENDS — Basic costume
ALL GIRL BAND REPRISE — Basic costume

PROPERTIES PLOT

FURNITURE
Desk
Three chairs
One small kiddy chair
Bench
Small table

PROPS
Trash:
Stick of gum — desk
Three large garish novels — two for Mindy, one for Stanley
Briefcase — Stanley

For Women Only:
Large book with ornate cover

Welcome to Kindergarten, Mrs. Johnson:
Handbag — Mrs. Johnson
Pig — cabinet
Evaluation — Ms. Thomas
Bad mother sign — Mrs. Thomas

Ms. Mae:
Magazine
Fan
Hairdressers cape
Towel
Tissue

Good Sports:
Four basketballs

Bluer Than You:
Letter of recommendation

Watching All the Pretty Young Men:
Three purses
Binoculars — Helen
Telescope — Helen
Fake money — Helen
Keys — Helen

French Song:
Beret
Cigaret holder
Cigarets

Hot Lunch:
Hardhat
Lunchbox with sandwich & cup

Emily the M.B.A.:
Four briefcases
Hubcap

Honeypot:
Hair flowers
Notepad
Pencil

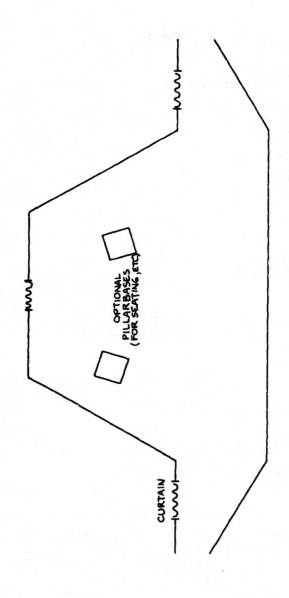

SCENE DESIGN

"A . . . MY NAME IS ALICE"

CURTAIN

OPTIONAL
PILLAR BASES
(FOR SEATING, ETC.)

THE MUSICAL OF MUSICALS (THE MUSICAL!)
Music by Eric Rockwell
Lyrics by Joanne Bogart
Book by Eric Rockwell and Joanne Bogart

2m, 2f / Musical / Unit Set

The Musical of Musicals (The Musical!) is a musical about musicals! In this hilarious satire of musical theatre, one story becomes five delightful musicals, each written in the distinctive style of a different master of the form, from Rodgers and Hammerstein to Stephen Sondheim. The basic plot: June is an ingenue who can't pay the rent and is threatened by her evil landlord. Will the handsome leading man come to the rescue? The variations are: a Rodgers & Hammerstein version, set in Kansas in August, complete with a dream ballet; a Sondheim version, featuring the landlord as a tortured artistic genius who slashes the throats of his tenants in revenge for not appreciating his work; a Jerry Herman version, as a splashy star vehicle; an Andrew Lloyd Webber version, a rock musical with themes borrowed from Puccini; and a Kander & Ebb version, set in a speakeasy in Chicago. This comic valentine to musical theatre was the longest running show in the York Theatre Company's 35-year history before moving to Off-Broadway.

"Witty! Refreshing! Juicily! Merciless!"
- Michael Feingold, *Village Voice*

"A GIFT FROM THE MUSICAL THEATRE GODS!"
– *TalkinBroadway.com*

"Real Wit, Real Charm! Two Smart Writers and Four Winning Performers! You get the picture, it's GREAT FUN!"
- *The New York Times*

"Funny, charming and refreshing!
It hits its targets with sophisticated affection!"
- *New York Magazine*

THE OFFICE PLAYS
Two full length plays by Adam Bock

THE RECEPTIONIST
Comedy / 2m., 2f. Interior

At the start of a typical day in the Northeast Office, Beverly deals effortlessly with ringing phones and her colleague's romantic troubles. But the appearance of a charming rep from the Central Office disrupts the friendly routine. And as the true nature of the company's business becomes apparent, The Receptionist raises disquieting, provocative questions about the consequences of complicity with evil.

"...Mr. Bock's poisoned Post-it note of a play."
- *New York Times*

"Bock's intense initial focus on the routine goes to the heart of *The Receptionist's* pointed, painfully timely allegory... elliptical, provocative play..."
- *Time Out New York*

THE THUGS
Comedy / 2m, 6f / Interior

The Obie Award winning dark comedy about work, thunder and the mysterious things that are happening on the 9th floor of a big law firm. When a group of temps try to discover the secrets that lurk in the hidden crevices of their workplace, they realize they would rather believe in gossip and rumors than face dangerous realities.

"Bock starts you off giggling, but leaves you with a chill."
- *Time Out New York*

"... a delightfully paranoid little nightmare that is both more chillingly realistic and pointedly absurd than anything John Grisham ever dreamed up."
- *New York Times*

SAMUELFRENCH.COM